B. J.-C.

Rhymes and Verses

B. J.-C.

Rhymes and Verses

ISBN/EAN: 9783337264239

Printed in Europe, USA, Canada, Australia, Japan

Cover: Foto ©Andreas Hilbeck / pixelio.de

More available books at **www.hansebooks.com**

RHYMES AND VERSES.

BY

J. C. B.

PRINTED FOR PRIVATE CIRCULATION ONLY.
1899.

PREFACE.

—◦◦◦—

If one should chance to look
　Within this little book
Who brings to it a criticising mind,
　He'll read—a little while;
　Then, with indulgent smile,
Will lay it down, for nought within he'll find.

CONTENTS.

CONTENTS

CONTENTS

ix

ERRATUM.

Page 109, line 6, *for* " building " *read* " adding."

THE CHRISTMAS TREE.

HURRAH for the merry, merry, merry Christmas tree,
With its gaudy tapers lighted, all as brilliant as can be,
And the happy children's faces, full of frolic and of glee,
As they dance and skip around the Christmas tree!

Hurrah for the laughing, daffing, chaffing company!
They come trooping, trooping, trooping, such a goodly
    sight to see—
Grannies, daddies, 'and the mammies, with the babies
    at their knee,
As they dance and skip around the Christmas tree.

Hurrah for the Christmas gifts, whatever they may be,
Whether dolls or woolly lambkins, china cups for drink-
    ing tea,
Hobby-horses or the little ships for those who love the sea—
So hurrah for Father Christmas and the tree!

Hurrah for the secrets held by that old Christmas tree—
The joyful happy whisperings, the wondrous mystery
That hangs o'er all these Christmas gifts kept under
    lock and key
Till the time arrives for all to come and see!

Alas for the merry, merry, merry Christmas tree!
For the memories around it, they will always cling to me;
For the parents who provided all the joy at Ferguslie.
To the mother's love we owe the Christmas tree.

CHRISTMAS DAY, 1898.

TIME was when Christmas Day to me
Was full, so very full, of glee
And love and charm and mystery;
      But that was long ago.
To-day old Christmas comes again,
Yet it is full of grief and pain;
Dear memories o'ercloud my brain,
      And cause sad tears to flow.

What joyful gath'rings round that tree
For many years—nigh fifty-three!
And I was always there to see—
      The happiest of them all.
To-day I have my Christmas spent
In reading o'er old letters sent
By loving hands—my mind intent
      On times beyond recall.

SAD THOUGHTS.

1898.

Sᴀᴅ thoughts come stealing round this Christmas night :
I scarce dare let them in to see the light.
Nay, rather I would turn them from the door,
And bid them come next year, but not before,
That so Time's healing wings may waft away
The darkest clouds, and bring the cheering day.
Then will I bid dear memories return
To sit beside my hearth, where brightly burn
With gentle warmth the pure and steady flames
Of lasting love, for those dear ones whose names
Are graven deep on heart and mind for aye.
So help me, memory, for a while to try
To banish sorrow.   Draw the portals to ;
Sleep on, till hopeful dawn the day renew.

PRAYER TO MEMORY.

FORSAKE me not, O Memory, while life lasts ;
Be with me when gray eve her shadows casts.
Thou hast the golden key that locks the door
On all I've seen, said, done—a varied store.
Keep all pent up that bring back grief and pain,
Yet set the others free that still remain ;
Draw up the curtain, let the scenes appear
That gave me joy each day, each month, each year ;
Let all the dearest faces of my youth
Arise before me, full of love and truth ;
Give me the power to know and name them all,
That I in fancy may my dear ones call ;
Then drop the curtain when the play is o'er,
Only to raise it on the heavenly shore.

LUNAR ECLIPSE.

AS SEEN FROM SKIDDAW ON DECEMBER 27, 1897.

OH, strange and wondrous sight, the moon's eclipse !
Describe it, ye who saw, with graphic lips,
How, watching long in vain, one blust'ry night,
Pale Cynthia still shone clear—superbly bright ;
At last, to wond'ring eyes a shade appears
Upon her eastern side, and slowly nears,
Cutting into the bright orb by degrees,
But half the surface still the gazer sees ;
The storm-clouds, hurrying past, forget to look
On this weird scene, engraved in Nature's book ;
The shadow stealthily engulfs the moon ;
A little longer—'twill be hidden soon.
The sighing winds impatient rush along,
Now roaring, and now moaning low in song ;
The darken'd moon still rides along the sky,
And earth lies veil'd beneath night's canopy.
What time the shade withdrew from Cynthia's face
The drifting clouds prevented further trace.

A STORM IN DECEMBER.

IN THE LAKE DISTRICT.

An evil spirit rushes through the breeze,
Tearing the branches of the tortured trees.
Descending from the mountain-side, it breaks
In angry gusts—the very ground it shakes.
The sullen lake is crested o'er with froth,
Bursting the narrow confines in its wrath ;
The stormy rain-clouds, scudding o'er the hills,
Descend like ropes of silver through the rills;
From black'ning skies, their sources duly fed,
They spring at last in fury from their bed.
Nor does the tempest slacken till in rage
It sweeps away the bridges at each stage
Along the highway, where the rivers flow
In frantic clamour to the lake below.

WINTER.

THE day is gone, the moon is pale and clear,
The landscape, wrapped in haze, looks dim and drear,
The evening air feels chill and raw and keen,
No trees nor hills nor houses near are seen ;
But standing looking from my open door,
A figure now I see, unseen before.

There, looming through the mist, a ghostly man
Comes creeping slowly on, as best he can :
Stern, aged, crusty, clad in snowy white,
His raiment soft and pure and shimmering white ;
Though old he seems, a steady course he'll steer,
His advent is inevitably near.

And nearer, yet more near, he comes apace ;
A frigid smile is on his wrinkled face,
His steely eyes look dim and hard and old,
His breath a vapour dense and damp and cold ;
I look upon his form so gaunt and thin,
And turning quickly, shut the door within.

He prowls around the house, but all in vain,
He tries an entrance everywhere to gain ;
On each small window-pane he coldly breathes,
A frosted diamond sparkling there he leaves.
I stir the fire, and pile it up with wood—
Old man and diamonds disappear for good.

The baffled foe soon beats a slow retreat ;
But quickly someone else he crawls to meet ;
It matters not to him, the first who comes
With breath of ice he suddenly benumbs ;
His victims fall before him by the score,
He greets them once, and lo ! they are no more.

Now, as I ponder deeply o'er these things,
And think of what this old man yearly brings
The mist, the frost, the snow, the diamond pane—
I now perceive, 'tis all to me quite plain,
His mantle white, his rigid aged frame,
I guess that WINTER surely is his name.

A BRILLIANT DAY AT UNDERSCAR.

At last a glorious day has dawn'd to cheer
Our wav'ring spirits, and the agèd year,
To make amends for tempests, thunder, rain
Hurl'd down in anger, deigns to smile again ;
The sun, resplendent, o'er the snow-clad hills
Shines on victorious, now the air he fills
With heat and spicy fragrance wafted down
From whiten'd mountain heights ; the distant town
Lies veil'd in mist, half hid the silent plain—
Or thus it seems from this remote domain.
The sharpen'd outlines of the hill-tops lie
Against the blue expanse of limpid sky ;
The frosts of yester-night have not decreased
The sound of waterfalls, nor have these ceased
To send their sparkling drops in silver streams,
To wander 'neath the glare of mid-day beams.
We breathe the sweet intoxicating air ;
" Oh, glorious day !" so brilliant and so rare !
A few short hours, and now the day declines ;

Encroaching twilight shades the soft'ning lines
Of golden splendour, margin'd round the height;
It overspreads the dark'ning land, and night
Descending slowly, covers with her wings
The sleeping vale, the lake, all living things.
The aged year has spent his ling'ring strength
To bless us with a perfect day at length.

December 30, 1898.

NEW YEAR'S EVE, 1898.

In storm and snow the old year cried "Adieu!"
Scarce calmed his rage till his last breath he drew;
Kind Nature, mindful of the new-born child,
Met him with clearing skies—with face that smiled.

I open wide the casement, and I hear
The midnight chimes ring in the glad New Year;
The snow-clad mountain peaks loom through the mist,
And by the moon's pale gleams are softly kissed;
The sleeping town lies hazy and remote,
Its valley thronged with clouds that ling'ring float,
Unwilling to resign their stormy reign,
To see the heir his peaceful kingdom gain.

Mists usher in the year, their veil withdrawn,
Clouds hover near, reluctant to be gone;
Like surly guardians of the realms of peace,
They bid the moon and stars their revels cease;
And, jealous of sweet Nature's radiant grace,
With sullen looks would all her joys efface.

BELATED SPRING.

And hast thou been so long in coming, Spring,
Only to carry hailstones on thy wing?
Hast thou so long with surly Winter fought,
Only to have thy vict'ry set at nought?
Thy rosy mornings full of promise bright
Nigh swallow'd up in long protracted night?
Thy flow'rets stirring in their mossy bed,
Must they have snow-drifts heaped upon their head?
Thy longings to bring forth to birth new life,
Must they be strangled in this chilly strife?
No! Nature can no longer bear to see
Her frozen nurslings die in misery;
She bids the cheering sun send forth his ray.
He comes, and just in time, to bring the day—
Reviving hope and heat in life benumbed
That must erelong have to its fate succumbed.

And now the reign of Night and Winter past,
Thy victory, O Spring, complete at last!
We greet thee joyfully, we shout and sing,
"Oh, live for ever, gay and happy Spring!"

We see thee crown thyself each day anew
With buds and blossoms fresh from morning dew ;
The fluffy fledgelings, chirping on the green
Attempt their timid flights with hops between ;
In meadows rich the sheep, with hungry greed,
On juicy grasses nibbling, hourly feed ;
The ewes seek shelter near the hedge from cold,
And lambs are daily added to the fold ;
The lowing calves, deprived of mother's care,
Scarce find the dewy herbs sufficient fare :
They watch the milkmaid coming with the pail
Of frothy milk—they never knew her fail ;
The foals are in the paddock by the rill—
Long legg'd, ungainly, frisking at their will ;
The browsing mare looks on—she's well content
To yield her sucklings their due nourishment.

The hedges, crown'd with fragrant wreaths of " May,"
Like snow showers out of season, deck the way.
All these most charming sights, and many more,
Thou bringest forth in time, from out thy store.
For all thy benefits we praises sing,
"Oh, live for ever, gay and happy Spring !"

EARLY SPRING IN THE LAKE DISTRICT.

'Twas a morning in April—I cannot forget,
For its dazzling brightness remains with me yet—
And the month had run on to the seventeenth day,
Just the time when young Spring loves to frolic and play;
I looked out of the window—how changed was the scene!
Ghostly mountains, white valleys, instead of the green;
Nearly up to the door a white carpet was spread,
And the lawn was wrapped up in a cold wintry bed.
The frail daffodil, rocking its poor fragile form
In a cradle of snowdrift, looked spent by the storm,
While the hyacinth, just peeping up from the ground,
Was nigh smothered in flakes; it could scarcely be found.

All at once o'er the land shone the sun, his kind face
In a moment illumined the desolate place:
He, with sparkling effusion, explained to us all
'Twas a frolic of Springtime to send this snowfall;
"You will see," he continued, "how fine the effect
On the mountains; the ridges are all new bedecked;

And how bracing the air ; see, all nature responds,
For grim Winter and Springtime are knit in fresh bonds :
Sympathetic, they each understand 'tis a play ;
Thus the coy maiden Spring chases Winter away ;
And while he, with feigned jealousy, gives her a push,
He besprinkles with snowflakes each tree, every bush."

But the lambs, in sad fright, have strayed out of the field,
And have crept to the shelter some hollow may yield ;
It is all very well for the seasons, no doubt,
Thus to flirt with each ether and gambol about ;
But 'tis death to the blossom on bush or on tree,
And it kills the first butterfly, nips the wild bee.
Then away, surly Winter, to some other land,
With your fun and your frolic and cold deadly hand !

ODE TO THE LARCH.

FAIR Lady Larch, how I have longed to see
Thy fragile form in vernal clothing clad!
Too long thy tender frame has stood disrobed,
A sport for lagging Winter's wildest moods.

Where is thy absent robing-maiden, Spring,
Who brings thee dainty garments year by year?
Long she has tarried past the "tiring" time,
Neglectful of her lady's pressing needs;
Yet I have seen her on the threshold oft;
Fain she would venture near, her genial face
Lit up with tender love and care for thee.
But surly Winter, guarding his domain,
Forbade her entrance, and with showers of hail
And snowflakes pelted her, till she, in haste,
Affrighted, fled: yet, as a mother's love
Would face the tiger's fury if he neared
Her sleeping babe, so Spring, undaunted, comes

2

Again, and yet again ; now weeping tears
Of soft seductive rain, now pleading rights
Infringed, and even feigning mirth, if by
This means she change the current of his wrath ;
But all of no avail, until at last
Hoar Winter, wearied of his frosty freaks,
Retires.
        And now, sweet Lady Larch, thou stand'st
Enwrapped in thy first robe of gossamer—
A dainty garb, and fresh, of tender green ;
And day by day thy happy maiden brings
A newer garment, diverse each in shade ;
Till, on this May-day morning, thou dost stand
Arrayed complete ; the crowning point of all—
A soft light tracery of pigmy plumes
Resembling fairy feathers.   This thy crown.

April, 1899.

A BREEZY MORNING.

Shimmer, shimmering in the breeze,
  Tossing arms from side to side,
There is mirth among the trees;
  Fast the clouds above them ride;
Shadows dance along the ground
To a sweet, low, sighing sound.

See them flitting o'er the wall;
  Phantom sprites, they lightly dance—
Now so large and now so small—
  Hither, thither, how they prance!
Blow, O wind, a merry blast,
Pipe a roundel, gay and fast.

Old King Sol has come to see,
  Beaming with benignant ray,
Cheering on the revelry;
  Much and oft he's pressed to stay,
For when he withdraws his light,
Then good-bye to every sprite!

FULL MOON.

THE moon will be full-faced to-night,
  Frail April nears an end ;
The lake will lie in cold clear light,
  The weather now will mend.
Look out and watch for Cynthia's crest,
Or ere you take yourself to rest.

She comes ! a bright bent line just peeps
  Above the dark hill brow ;
Faster and faster still she creeps—
  She shines a full moon now.
The sleeping valleys far below
Lie undisturbed, but feel the glow.

Come out ! 'tis waste of time to sit
  By fires and candlelight
While Nature has her garden lit
  With lamps of clearest light ;
The air is filled with calm so deep,
'Twill aid our rest and send us sleep.

April, 1899.

THE EARLY RISERS.

One April morn I chanced to wake
  Just at the break of day—
A dim blue light was on the lake,
  The hills were cold and gray ;
The trees stood still in silence deep,
  Not one small leaflet stirred ;
The land was wrapped profound in sleep,
  And this is what I heard :

A conversation sweet and low,
  In little twittering notes,
A murmuring talk in constant flow
  From dainty little throats :
A hundred questions met replies,
  And all in full accord ;
The cadence seemed to fall and rise—
  Each one put in a word.

What might the council contemplate
  Remains a mystery—
May they decide in this debate
  To build on every tree !

And may our ivy-coloured wall
Beguile them there to nest !
Then I shall hear them when they call
Their mates to come to rest.

A RAINY DAY.

A SOAKING scene presents itself to-day,
A sorry prospect for the month of May;
A dreary outlook for the village queen
Who dreams of May-day frolics on the green;
A chilling welcome to the week-old lamb,
Just struggling to its feet beside its dam;
To fledgeling hopping from the cosy nest,
Bedrenched in raindrops hanging from its breast.

The peacock droops his once proud glorious tail
Forlorn, in shelter o'er veranda rail;
The lake lies wrapt in many a misty shower;
The tell-tale weather-glass falls every hour;
The sheep, resigned, lie on the soaking grass
With heads upraised—they think the rain may pass;
For now a clearing in the sky betrays
The near approach of Sol's all-cheerful rays.

APRIL'S FAREWELL.

OH, what a day ! a perfect April day !
Thus fly the happy words from happy lips
Scarce wakened from the morning's sleep refreshed ;
And what a picture lies before us spread !
A morning feast to open wide the eyes,
And fill the cup of calm content full up.

In earlier years our hearts had danced for joy ;
Now sober, slower heart-beats do not leap,
Yet quicken into grateful gladness still,
To see the brilliant glory of this day—
A day to be remembered—set against
A hundred days of drizzling mist and weeks
Made drear by storm.   We drink deep draughts this morn
Of Nature's bounty—yet the cup is full !

The mountains stand clear-cut against the blue ;
Their varied peaks, their rounded tops, their slopes,
Their hollows and their crests patched here and there

With larch's vivid green.   Deep shadows move
In motion with the drift of April clouds
That glide across the blueness of the sky.

This day the fickle month bids us farewell;
To-morrow May steps in, and all frail things—
The lambs, the chicks, the feathered young unborn,
Just opening the shell—with boldness now
Will venture forth to greet sweet smiling May.
Yet April's parting touch—a touch of frost—
Has nipped the morning air; but all is still:
Nought do I hear, save pigeon's cooing note
Down in the wood, the cuckoo's call, the thrush
In animated converse with his mate,
Now sweet and low, now vivid and intense;
This breaks the silence, which, thus broken, seems
More restful and more pleasing than before.

April, 1899.

EARLY OPEN-AIR WORSHIP, SUNDAY MORNING.

A Sabbath stillness lies upon the land,
All nature feels the day of rest at hand ;
The hills more solemn look, benign they lie
In all the fulness of their majesty.

The lake, profound, and in reflective mood,
Repeats the clouds, the hills, the leafy wood ;
The rigid trees their graceful movements cease,
They stand stern guardians of the Sabbath peace.

The fragrant blooms, distilled in soothing balm,
Shed sweetest incense o'er the sacred calm ;
All things inanimate in worship rise,
They call us to consider and be wise !

Unconsciously we bend and, silent, pray
For hearts to feel the goodness of the day ;
Kind thoughts crowd on us, good in all we find ;
Peace steals upon us and uplifts the mind.

With hope and strength renewed, we look around,
And lo ! on every side new light is found ;
It shines upon our ways—'tis from above ;
We kneel to Nature's God—His name is Love !

May, 1899.

MUTINOUS MAY.

O MAY, you've disappointed us!
We thought to see you leap and spring
To summer heat, and blossoms bring
To scatter with a careless fling
O'er tree, o'er lawn, o'er everything—
And now you've disappointed us!

We thought to see you glorious
In all your radiant colours dight,
And by your name-child clothed in white,
In lilac cloaked, capped in sunlight,
To greet our eager, wistful sight;
But now you've disappointed us!

We thought to find you riotous,
In scented breeze from sweetest flower,
In hum of bees on blooming bower,
Wafting fresh fragrance every hour—
Such summer wealth should be your dower;
But, May, you've disappointed us!

We woke to find you furious,
With scowling face, and drenched in tears,
And all your work is in arrears;
No wonder, then, you have your fears;
Your reputation's gone for years—
For much you've disappointed us!

May, 1899.

JOYOUS JUNE.

You are coming very soon,
        Joyous June ;
You will bring the flowers sweet,
You will lay them at our feet ;
You will shake the blossom free
From the pear and apple tree,
        Joyous June.

You are coming none too soon,
        Leafy June ;
For the sunshine has been rare,
For the ash-tree still is bare ;
You will set the hawthorn-tree
'Neath a snow-white broidery,
        Leafy June.

You will sing a merry tune,
        Rosy June ;
You will steal with balmy air
To our hearts, and lift our care ;

JOYOUS JUNE

You will trip, and you will dance,
You shall every joy enhance,
    Rosy June.

You will make the whole day noon,
    Sunny June ;
You will carry in your hand
Roses rare to deck the land ;
You will banish chilly May ;
She has had her dreary day,
    Sunny June.

May 28, 1899

A SUMMER CALM.

ON LAND AND WATER.

AT last our weary longing eyes
  Bid welcome to belated summer,
And visions of sweet June arise—
  Make way, chill May, for the new-comer !
The scent of fresh-mown grass, the flowers,
  The brooklet's near and soothing murmur,
The busy birds that haunt the bowers
  Catch at my heart and bind it firmer.

Sweet hawthorn, thou too soon wilt fade,
  Thy snow-white blooms will tan and wither ;
Oh, could short summer but have stayed
  Till I be free to come back hither !
Blithe blackbirds fill the day with song,
  Green branches underneath them quiver,
Swaying beneath the choral throng
  While they their melody deliver.

All nature now is lulled to sleep ;
  The smallest leaf is void of motion ;
And ships lie slumb'ring on the deep,
  Their shadows mirror'd in the ocean.
Limp sea-gulls, clustered on the shore,
  At our approach make vast commotion,
And, screaming to the air, they soar
  To kiss the cloudlets with devotion.

The sea reflects their sudden flight,
  And, shimmering, laughs in pure derision ;
To woo the cloudlets from their heights,
  O sea-gull, cannot be thy mission !
Sweet-scented land, soft-painted sea,
  If I were asked which is the fairest,
My answer thus, and thus should be :
  "Compare them, thou, an' if thou darest !"
For both are perfect in their way ;
  In truth, I know not which is rarest—
Thou, limpid sea, or earth so gay,
  Whose image on thy breast thou bearest.

June 1, 1899.

THE SUMMER DAY.

THE lights upon the sky,
The swallows soaring high,
The shadows flitting by
    In summer heat.

The rush of streamlet small,
The roar of waterfall,
The silent river's roll
    Where waters meet.

Sweet scents upon the breeze,
The rustling of the trees,
The humming of the bees
    Make music sweet.

With open eye and ear
For all we see and hear,
In Nature's mirror clear,
    These joys we greet.

Such pleasures we enjoy,
Delights without alloy
Which nothing can destroy
    In our retreat.

A SUNNY DAY WASTED.

How bright is the sunshine, how glad is the day!
How fleeting the moment!—'twill soon pass away;
Already a cloudlet appears in the sky,
The harbinger sure of a storm that is nigh.

Then lay down your writing, come out to the door;
You'll see for yourself what I told you before—
The sunshine is fleeting, oh, hasten, I pray!
Oh, waste not the gladness of this precious day!

There's time and to spare for the rhyme and the pen;
When rain-clouds sweep down, we'll have full leisure then;
Too soon 'twill be ev'ning, so fast goes the time:
Come! come! I've no patience, not even for rhyme!

The storm-cloud is gath'ring, and now it is near,
With thunder and downpour, 'twill drench us, I fear;
See! see! 'tis upon us, and now 'tis too late:
The day is quite wasted; how sad is our fate!

A FABLE OF THE CLOUDS.

WHILE walking in my garden one fine day,
I heard a plaintive voice behind me say :
"Alas ! this cruel heat I cannot bear !
Oh for some shelter from the sun's fierce glare !"
I turned, and saw a flower upon its stalk,
Hang drooping near the margin of the walk ;
And while I gazed, it fell upon the ground.
I stood amazed, for lo ! thence came the sound !

Just then a cloudlet rose upon the sky,
And, list'ning, seemed to hear the flower's sad cry ;
Its fleecy veil athwart the sun it trailed,
And wept a few soft tears, then lightly sailed
Above the dying flower, and loitered there,
Bedewing with cool drops the petals rare.
The flower, reviving, lifted up its head,
And to the cloud in grateful accents said :

" O friend, whoe'er you be that succour bring
To such as I, a poor frail dying thing,

I bless and thank you from my inmost heart ;
I pray that you may never hence depart.
Oh, stay, and with your gentle dews revive
A drooping flower that cannot long survive,
Unless your kindly aid you will extend,
To prove yourself a true and constant friend !"

" I cannot linger now," the cloud replied,
" For other suppliants must not be denied,
Who wait my cooling shade and fresh'ning showers
To bring them back to health, renew their powers ;
But see ! look up ! I carry in my train
Innumerable clouds foretelling rain ;
Like mimic ships in sail, they drift with speed.
I do not leave you friendless in your need !"

Thus saying, and anon with breezy haste,
The cloud now floated on, no time to waste,
When spying in a field some drop-ripe grain,
That, drooping on its stalk, was somewhat lain,
With philanthropic zeal a blast it sent
Upon the waving corn with good intent.
Alas! this act, with indiscretion fraught,
Much sad destruction caused from want of thought.

The full ripe grain, recoiling from the shake,
First trembled, then with fear began to quake ;

And falling from its sheath upon the ground,
Was lost to sight, nor ever would be found
But by the feathered tribe who hover there
When coming harvests shall the fields lay bare ;
The emptied stalks in anger waved and tossed
Their heads, for all their wealth was spilt and lost.

Now, rustling in their rage, in accents hoarse
Expostulations tendered they with force.
"What means this rude intrusion ?" then they cried.
" Have we not months of wind and rain defied,
And slowly ripened 'neath the tardy sun ?
Now all our care and labour are undone.
O ruthless cloud, this is a sorry jest
Of all our cherished hopes us to divest !"

" No jest was meant," now came the meek reply ;
" In all good faith I earnestly did try
To cool your heated heads.   You seemed athirst—
Your over-ripened grain the husks had burst ;
But now, I fear, my services have led
To ruin and disaster dire instead.
A lesson from your anger I will learn :
When giving help, first always to discern
The proper ways and means with tact to use ;
The times and seasons too most fit to choose !"

THE FABLE OF THE WOODS.

Now Autumn had grown old when this occurred—
While sitting in the woods I overheard
The gossip of the trees at close of day ;
The Pine-tree to the Chestnut sang her lay :
" I am surprised, my friend, you should appear
In such a costume, at this time of year.
How long do you suppose those robes will last,
And winter coming near so very fast ?

" One touch of frost, and all your wealth of gold
Will fall, and leave you shivering in the cold ;
Your foliage, so delicately bright,
Is quite unfitted with the winds to fight ;
Your garments you have changed already thrice ;
In dainty buds of Spring you did look nice.
Your summer green was so becoming, too,
Why change again to robes of richer hue ?
Your spiral blooms of white so pure, they were
Most comely of the mantles you did wear.

Extravagance your weakness is, I see,
'Twill lead you into abject poverty.
The shaken fruit, just fallen from your lap,
Ought now, at harvest, to be garnered up ;
Like unripe apples scattered on the ground,
By wayside travellers soon they will be found.
A bad example to your friends you show—
You, being nobler, surely ought to know
That winter has no other dress in store
For Lime-tree, Ash, Oak, Birch or Sycamore ;
So, like you, having squandered all their wealth,
Regardless of their comfort and their health,
In cold and nakedness they soon will stand
Till spring comes round again to deck the land.

" Your vanity is nurtured, I dare say,
By artists who in autumn often stray
Along these woodland paths to catch the tints,
From dying summer's lips to get some hints ;
They put your vivid colours on their brush,
Their praises of your beauty make me blush.
Yet I, who always look my very best,
Cannot with your inconstancy contest.
Although with strict economy I can
Afford to gratify the eye of man
By wearing my best gown the winter through,
My cheerful sameness cannot cope with you.

Yet this I know—the time will surely come
When icy breezes will your limbs benumb;
Then you would gladly all your pride demean
To sell your birthright to an evergreen."

And now the Rhododendron up and spake :
" O Pine, your judgment I incline to take.
My robes, like yours, appear for ever new,
Enlivened by fresh tips of green, 'tis true,
And in the summer time, I must confess,
My blossoms make a most enchanting dress ;
Yet, after they are gone, I'm wrapped from cold
In verdure rich, that never can grow old.
I certainly disdain the foolish pride
That casts all garments carelessly aside."

The Chestnut, having listened to the end,
Her character now hastened to defend.
" I cannot boast," said she, " your constancy,
Your leafage, never failing in supply ;
I am but what kind Nature deems is best ;
I hear her voice, to her I leave the rest ;
To her the ordering of my garb I leave ;
Her taste is finer than I could conceive.
And when in her good time she gives command
That I in winter nakedness should stand
Denuded, yet I murmur not—I know
'Tis that my beauty greater still may grow."

Thus said the Chestnut, and the other trees
All murmured their approval through the breeze,
Except the Rhododendron and the Pine,
Whose arguments took quite another line.
I left them then to settle their dispute
Among themselves, for it had taken root.
" I should not wonder if some other day
The contest were renewed," I heard them say.

OCTOBER.

October, richest month of all the year !
With summer left behind and winter near,
Thou bring'st the golden harvest in thy train
Of russet leaves, bright seeds, belated grain.
Thy Indian summer days, more glorious far
Than brightest suns of June and July are.
No other season can with thee compare,
So rich the regal garments thou dost wear !

At early morn a bath of silver dew
Does all thy beauty and thy strength renew ;
And now, arrayed at noon in garments bright,
Thy mellow Autumn tints are bathed in light.
Thy crowning glory is the evening dress,
The flowing robe of flaming gorgeousness,
The glossy raiment fleck'd amidst the sheen,
With golden patches flung on mossy green.

Rich coral beads, embroidered here and there,
And purple jewels clustered in thy hair
Complete a toilet fit for any queen,
And crown thee monarch of the glorious scene !

But not alone to lavish on thyself
Dost thou display this show of all thy wealth ;
A little child, with basket on her arm,
Can pluck thy tempting fruit, and think no harm.
The songsters of the woods, with clear soft pipe,
They sweetly chirp their thanks for berries ripe.
Thy bounteous hand thou stretchest out to all—
On every living creature blessings fall.
October, richest month of all the year !
We thank thee for thy beauty, thy good cheer !

THE UNLUCKY BEAR.

I was sitting one morning, intent on my book,
When a noise through the window aroused me to look ;
'Twas a man with a horn, and he blew such a blast,
" Now," methought, " a fine coach with four horses has
    passed."

But not so ; it was only a huge muzzled bear,
That was standing erect, with a pitiful air ;
Then, with slow shuffling steps, he came painfully by,
Yet he dared not relax from his posture—and why ?

In the hand of his leader a long wooden pole
Was the sign of the taskmaster's rigid control ;
While, with frequent reminders, he stopped at each door,
The long pole was employed to elicit a roar.

Soon they passed from the window, and out of my sight ;
But it happened I took a short stroll that same night,
And I saw a small crowd in a neighbouring street—
Here, alas ! was poor Bruin on tottering feet !

All the day, and each hour, he had walked through the town,
Till at last, on all-fours, he came staggering down ;
Yet he still, at a sign from the pole, raised his paws :
Had he known his own strength, he had raised his ten claws !

OUR BULLFINCH.

I HAVE a bullfinch prisoned in a cage—
His plumes are varied neither more nor less
Than others of his kind ; his cap is black,
His vest a russet red, his coat is gray,
His tail is sable—wings are sable tipped.

Such is my bird. Dainty and neat he is
To outward sight, but this is smallest praise.
His ways intelligent ; affection deep
Lies in that little fluffy breast ; he knows,
He loves his friends, and puts forth all his powers
Of heart and voice to welcome them. My step
He seems to know ere I come into sight ;
Scarce have I crossed the threshold of the door
Ere his clear shout of gladness fills the room ;
Then, when I near his cage, he pipes his tunes—
The simple airs he learnt ere he was mine.
His black cap, rising, with the cadence falls
In equal motion with his tail, which moves
In measured numbers to the music sweet.

Such is my bullfinch ; always in his joy
He pipes to me, but to my husband shows
Another mood—with him he fights, in love ;
Not anger moves him, 'tis a playful freak,
As who should say : " You are my playmate—you ;
Come, let us see who is the better man !"

Such is our little friend, in glad content,
If only we are near him in the room ;
But when we rise to go, a plaintive chirp
Arrests us ere we reach the door.   Almost
With faltering steps, regretful, we depart—
Such is the power of love in things so small.

THE SHEPHERD'S MISTAKE.

THERE is sorrow to-day in the flock,
  There is bleating, and wonder and woe;
Some are standing as still as a rock,
  One is wandering, wild, to and fro.

She is seeking, and seeking, for what?
  She has trotted all over the ground;
She has sought through the field, every spot,
  But her lambkin is not to be found.

Till at last, by some chance, she descries
  A lone spot just behind the old yew,
And a something there motionless lies—
  Still it lies, though its dam comes in view.

With a bleat of endearment and joy,
  The fond mother trots up to her young;
Cruel fate! her fond hopes to destroy;
  For 'tis on a dead thing they are hung.

And the shepherd had noticed this lamb;
  To marauders it might fall a prey,
Since it oft did not run with its dam,
  But more often beside her it lay.

On the hill lives the fox, and its lair
  Almost neighbours the fold of the flock,
And it scents out its prey, even there
  Midst the heather and whinbush and rock.

To protect this weak lamb from its foe
  By fleece-tarring the shepherd had meant;
But how then could the poor mother know
  Her own lambkin, if not by the scent?

And the frail thing oft crept to her side,
  Yet she would not allow its approach;
All the nourishment needful denied;
  Not one inch would she let it encroach.

There is sorrow to-day in the flock,
  There is bleating, and wonder and woe;
Some are standing as still as a rock;
  One is wandering, wild, to and fro.

She is seeking, and seeking, for what?
  She has trotted all over the ground;
She has sought through the field, every spot;
  Still her lambkin is not to be found.

A WALK WITH OUR FAITHFUL COLLIE "SCOTT."

Come hither, Scott, we'll sally forth ;
　　I'll just go fetch my hat.
Alas ! though reared with care from birth,
　　You're growing much too fat !

We may not venture by the lake,
　　'Tis too far down below ;
Then what direction can we take,
　　And whither shall we go ?

I know what you would wish to say,
　　If only you could tell—
"We'll walk upon the hill to-day,
　　Midst heath and sweet bluebell.

" For there the bunnies sport about,
　　Amuse me very much."
They're very funny things, no doubt ;
　　But mind, you must not touch !

Come, come, good sir, restrain your joy;
  How shrill and loud your bark !
You're very happy now, good boy ;
  But stay, just isten—hark !

I hear the bleating of the sheep ;
  We must not go too near.
You fain would have one little peep ;
  You'd startle them, I fear.

For sheep are timid things, you know,
  They're stupid too, and shy ;
Your bushy tail would scare them so,
  If we were passing by.

Good dog ! I know your gentle way :
  You'd turn your head aside
If any lambkins chanced to stray,
  Or, trembling, tried to hide.

Now run, old Scott, go lie amid
  The grass and bracken tall ;
Be off, sir, do as you are bid !
  You scare them one and all.

Keep back, keep back ! we've come too near !
  They're off in sudden fright ;
How cunningly you're hidden here !
  Your head's quite out of sight !

4—2

Then why in terror do they rush ?
Lie still—oh, do not stir !
They see you just behind the bush ;
Your tail betrays you, sir !

Oh, why do sheep on hilltops roam ?
I'm sure I cannot say ;
But this I know—we must go home,
They've spoilt our sport to-day.

THE BUTTERFLY.

There he is, sitting
   Where the thorn blows ;
Now he is flitting,
   Onward he goes.

Where will he wander,
   Whither his flight ?
Down into yonder
   Garden of light.

There he finds daisies,
   Softest of seats ;
Lost in sweet mazes,
   Fairies he greets.

Lurking in posies,
   Blooms of the best ;
There he reposes,
   Sinking to rest.

Softly enfolding
  Wings pearly white,
To the leaves holding
  During the night.

When the sun rouses
  Warbler and bee
Out of their houses,
  Forth cometh he.

Butterfly, frailest
  Of living things,
Touch all the palest
  Blooms with your wings,

To their hearts sending
  Flashes of light,
On your way wending
  Far from our sight,

Leaving a token
  Summer is near,
Winter is broken,
  Springtime is here.

Butterfly, hasten
  Back to the thorn,
Cold hearts to chasten—
  Hearts all forlorn.

Teach them to sorrow
  Only for sin ;
Tell them to-morrow
  They may begin,

Gratefully joying
  In the glad hours,
Long days employing
  Gathering flowers,

Dull eyes to brighten
  With the sweet bloom,
Sad hearts to lighten, ;
  And lift from their gloom.

"CHIPS."

I KNOW a dog, his name is Chips,
  His appetite is keen ;
For cakes and sweets he licks his lips,
  And yet he's very lean.

Poor little Chips, he's grown so light
  In searching for his prey ;
He scours the plain from morn to night,
  He runs about all day.

The heather tall, with lilac hue,
  Grows strong and dense around ;
'Tis like a purple sea in view,
  It overspreads the ground.

Chips sniffs about, and burrows there,
  He bounds along with glee ;
He scents a rabbit everywhere,
  He's never tired—not he !

One morning from my window high
   Behold, a skulking thief!
The wretched dog I now descry
   Come slinking through the heath.

A rabbit in his mouth he bears,
   In secret to devour—
Flesh, skin and bones with greed he tears;
   He's ill that very hour.

To rabbits Chips now shows distaste,
   But still he can't consent
His opportunities to waste,
   He'll hunt some other scent.

Down in the hollow, deep and still,
   A sleepy lakelet lies;
Around this lake Chips roams at will,
   A rat at last he spies.

O Chips, how can you condescend
   To stalk such horrid game?
A taste so low you must amend,
   Or you will come to shame!

So back he creeps, with downcast mien,
   Ashamed to tell his woes;
For not one brace of rats has been
   In reach of Chippie's nose.

A sadder and a wiser dog,
 He soon retires to rest ;
He seldom now looks near a bog—
 The chase has lost its zest.

THE OLD PONY.

" Take your ease, enjoy your day
In the paddock, while you may."

Poor old pony, there you lie,
Little knowing you must die
Ere the summer scarce is run,
Or your leisure has begun ;
For you carried many a load
O'er a rough and hilly road.

Now the " vet." has come from town,
Saying, " You must put him down,
Since the pony is so old,
And the winters here are cold.
Cruel kindness it would be,
Leaving him at liberty,
Slowly freezing to his death,
Sighing out his latest breath ;
Starving, for his teeth are gone,
And there's nought to feed upon.
So, before September's close,
He must take his long repose !"

Pony, fate is hard on you ;
Faithful you have been, and true.
Some amends we thought to make,
Poor old pony ! for your sake ;
And we put you in the field
That the richest grass does yield,
There to sun yourself at ease,
Doing nought but what you please.
Should the summer linger long,
Pony, would it make you strong ?

Yet, if that is not to be,
If there's nought but misery
Waiting for you here below,
Pony, we must let you go ;
But let Nature name the day,
Gently leading you away.

THE COMMON HOUSE-FLY.

WILL no one have pity upon the house-fly?
An innocent creature with sharpness of eye,
At times a great nuisance, I cannot deny,
Yet take some compassion upon the house-fly.

Misfortune o'ertakes him where'er he may crawl;
To heights he may clamber, but if he should fall,
Hard fingers await him, though tiny and small,
To press and impale him—most cruel of all!

For cruelty lurks in the heart of a child;
The mother looks on, to the play reconciled.
She says, in soft accents, so weak and so mild,
" He kills ALL the flies, darling boy, he's so wild!"

Yet, parents, bethink you, there will come a day
Of reck'ning for you, and for which you must pay;
For the child that rejoices these poor flies to slay
Will not scruple to break your own heart in his play.

Then let the house-fly your compassion awake,
If only because of his constancy's sake ;
His habit of clinging he never will break,
Nor through the long winter his friends can forsake.

Then into odd corners he slowly will creep,
To fall into slumbers profound and so deep
That nought does disturb him, so dead is his sleep,
Till captured by maids with their brooms when they sweep.

A PARROT FOR SALE.

A PARROT, a parrot for sale !
A bird with a fine scarlet tail ;
  His sleek plumage is gray
On his back and his wing ;
  He is wise, he is gay,
He can talk, he can sing.
A parrot, a parrot for sale !

'Twould take hour upon hour to retail
All his virtues, each one in detail ;
  In the morning he sings,
He wakes us from sleep,
  And, oh, how his voice rings !
It is high, it is deep.
A parrot, a parrot for sale !

" Three cheers for the Queen !" is his wail ;
His mimicry never would fail ;
  But his politics change,
They go much with the times,
  So they have a wide range
To fit in with his rhymes—

"Three cheers for Lord Salisbury!"
"Three cheers for Lord Rosebery!"
A parrot, a parrot for sale!

Such praises will surely prevail,
If still to convince you I fail,
    And I see in your eye,
Though your voice is so mute,
    You would fain ask me why—
You've a question to put—
WHY this parrot, THIS parrot's for sale!

To be frank, there's a fault I bewail—
Thereby hangs a moral and tale:
    When to breakfast we come
Poll shrieks out a salute;
    We're at once stricken dumb,
For the shock is acute—
A parrot, a parrot for sale!

The grief that one fault may entail
Is enough to make moralists quail,
    Since for this single trick
We must part with our pet,
    So amusing, so quick,
To our lasting regret.
A parrot, a parrot for sale!

MY LADY'S COMPANION.

My lady has a friend
　Of whom she never tires,
Whom she consults times without end,
　And whom she much admires.

At morn, when she awakes,
　And when she goes to rest,
Much council with her friend she takes,
　This friend whom she loves best.

With her she roams about,
　Where'er her wand'rings lead—
To promenade, or dance, or rout,
　Companion true indeed!

Upon her face she'll look
　As oft she gets the chance,
In every quiet place and nook,
　And after every dance.

5

And yet this friend so true,
　Though beautiful her face,
She ne'er by chance comes into view,
　But in her proper place.

My lady could not find
　With idle hours to pass
A friend more suited to her mind—
　Her pocket looking-glass !

WINIFRED.

O WINIFRED, child Winifred!
　It passes me to know
What wisdom lurks in that small head,
　Your moods do vary so;
For when you sit beside me, child,
　And look into my face,
I see no hint of gambols wild,
　So full of youthful grace.

Your speaking eye is grave with thought,
　Your restless hands are still,
Your mind is busy: "Have they brought
　My pony from the hill?
For every night he must be housed,
　My lambkin, too, be led
Out from the field whereon she browsed,
　To shelter in the shed."

Then, in a twinkling, with a bound,
　You flutter from your seat,
Up on the hill, with ne'er a sound,
　Now speed your anxious feet;

And hark! a joyful bleat is heard,
  The tethered lamb has seen
From far her mistress, like a bird,
  Come flitting o'er the green.

Fast down the heather-scented hill
  The happy pair are led,
Both bound to follow at your will,
  By love's strong silken thread.
"Good-night, my pets!" I hear you cry,
  As, with a parting glance,
Returning by the path, you fly,
  And o'er the threshold dance.

O child, with woman's heart and mind!
  We fain would have you stand
Forever thus—young, wise, and kind,
  Upon the borderland,
Betwixt the budding and the bloom,
  Shedding upon life's way
A fragrant joy dispelling gloom,
  And brightening our day.

PALE PHYLLIS.

PALE Phyllis moves with ease and grace,
She walks with grave and earnest face,
Swaying in meditative pace,
   Her figure lithe and tall.
Beneath her garden wall she strays,
Where lovely roses interlace;
Their rich profusion leaves no space
   On that old crumbling wall.

With gentle, slender finger-tips
She lifts each rose up to her lips,
Inhaling fragrance while she sips
   Delight from every flower;
And fondly ling'ring over each,
Her eager eyes almost beseech
The blooms to bend within her reach,
   While higher still they tower.

What does she murmur to the rose,
While, slowly loit'ring, on she goes?
Is it a blessing she bestows?
    So softly does she pass.
See, from her robe she takes a toy,
And lifts it up with look so coy,
While to her face she holds with joy
    A small round looking-glass!

Now Phyllis plucks a bloom with care,
And deftly bends it on her hair
With her complexion to compare—
    The pale pink blushing rose.
" They suit me—yes, they cannot fail;
They well become my face so pale.
These lovely blossoms, pure and frail,
    I am content with those."

A basket from her arm she takes,
And one by one the stems she breaks
Of twenty roses like snowflakes;
    She fills it to the brim.
The poor dismantled rose-tree stands,
Despoiled of all its blooms by hands
Made cruel by the vain demands
    Of this most selfish whim.

She decks her bodice and her hair,
The fragrance fills the ev'ning air ;
She knows herself a woman fair,
      Yet stifles she a sigh.
And forth she steps with sad, cold pride ;
A brimming tear she tries to hide.
What woe can this fair maid betide ?
      She weeps—but tell me why ?

She mingles with companions gay,
For this has been a gala-day,
But now no longer will she stay,
      Though yet the night is young.
The dying roses on her breast,
She has to them her grief confessed,
When homeward bent, in mind distressed,
      All tearful and unstrung.

" My vanity has been my bane ;
It has my sweetest roses slain.
In former years I would disdain
      Such wanton waste and wreck ;
And now my grief has dulled the day
That opened glad and bright and gay.
No more shall I my roses slay,
      My waving hair to deck."

MY TRUE FRIEND.

I HAVE a friend I seldom see,
A dear good friend she is to me ;
By kinship—cousin in degree,
   Yet sister true at heart.
Together we in childhood played,
And oft she gave me kindly aid
When, idling, I the task delayed
   In which I took my part.

To school together we were sent,
With lagging feet our steps were bent
In duty's path, our minds up-pent
   In thoughts of sport and play.
Arrived at last, our seats we took,
Composed our mien with serious look,
And soon were deep in slate and book
   Till slow advanced mid-day.

Then quick and frolicsome we hied
Our favoured nook none else had spied,
And there quite snugly we did hide,
   And frisk the hour away.
Ah me! what happy times were those!
I'll ne'er forget them till life's close;
Through wealth of joys or midst of woes
    They yet with me will stay!

Long years have passed, we're growing old,
And yet our friendship is not cold,
Oft to each other we unfold
   Our hopes, our fears, our joy.
Though many miles our homes divide—
She seaward, I in town reside—
Our thoughts still meet, nor time nor tide
   Can comradeship destroy.

MY LITTLE BESS.

How winsome is my little Bess!
  She chatters all the day;
But what she means you'll never guess,
  She has so much to say.

Her toddling feet are running yet,
  She runs from morn to night;
She must be tired, my bonny pet,
  Yet she is gay and bright.

I cannot make her go to bed,
  The naughty little queen;
She storms and shakes her curly head.
  " You rogue, what do you mean ?

" The little birds have gone to rest
  Beneath their ivy roof;
They're tuck'd into their cosy nest;
  They've needed no reproof.

" So come, you naughty lisping thing,
  And nestle in my arm.
Come, fold your soft and pretty wing;
  I'll keep you from all harm."

TOMMY DODD.

I HAVE a tiny rod
For little Tommy Dodd;
I bought it when abroad,
    And 'tis in pickle now.

He may not want it yet,
But when he's in a pet,
I say it with regret,
    I fear we'll have a row.

For Tommy is a boy
Who gives us all great joy,
And yet he may annoy—
    A little tyrant, he!

Imperious Tommy Dodd!
He's quite a tiny god;
He gives a little nod,
    Slaves bow on bended knee.

MERRY MAISIE.

MERRY little Maisie,
  Frolicsome and gay,
Dainty as a daisy,
  Six years old to-day.

Mocking little Maisie,
  Brimming o'er with fun,
None can call you lazy,
  Ever on the run.

Never still one minute,
  Lessons not begun,
Energy infinite,
  Pretty, naughty one!

Every precious moment
  Spent in pranks and play;
Saucy, tiny torment,
  Born to disobey!

Time is coming surely,
  Holding in his hands
Fortunes tied securely,
  Bound with silver bands.

And when he discloses
  What he's got for you,
May a path of roses
  Meet your eyes so blue.

THE AGED POSTMAN.

YEAR after year he wends his weary way,
Through storm and tempest on the bleakest day,
Through pelting rain, and drifting snow and sleet,
On roads ice-bound, unsafe for stumbling feet.

His daily toil through winter, this, and when
The season rounds to spring and summer, then
His soul revives to meet the warmer days,
His limbs feel stronger on the steep highways,
The task comes easier to his feeble gait,
Nor does fulfilment on his weakness wait.
He strains his utmost up the weary road ;
Arrives in time, sore spent, with heavy load.
Oppressed with heat, he pants up to the door—
'Tis his last work ; he carries mails no more.

Again spring smiles on the advancing year,
On sorrowing hearts, by loss of friends made sere ;
They feel the glow, but find it not akin
To all the desolation pent within.

Thus feels the lonely man, of love bereft;
To him his home now desolate is left.
The wife, companion of her aged spouse
For fifty years, has passed from hearth and house.
And he is left, yet mercy guides his fate—
A daughter's love and care upon him wait;
But, drooping day by day, he lingers on,
All hope and pleasure in his life are gone.

April, 1899.

LILY LORIMER.

Oh, sweet Lily Lorimer, fresh as the dew !
She's happy, she's winsome, she's modest and true,
She's blithe as the mavis that carols all day ;
Her presence is welcóme as flow'rets in May.

Then live on, sweet Lily, in youth ever new!
In hope and in gladness that nought can subdue,
To lighten our hearts—we are fast growing old—
To warm with thy radiance the lives that are cold.

For Time, the sad reaper, cannot be defied ;
But Lily, our darling, to him is denied.
He may steal the fair casket, if such be his will,
But our jewel enshrined in our hearts he can't kill !

Live on, Lily Lorimer, fresh as the dew ;
We fear no sad partings from friends such as you !
Though fortune should part us, and fate prove unkind,
Your spirit, still present, will keep us resigned.

WISE LITTLE WINNIE.

LITTLE Winnie, the child of our neighbour next door,
Was the wisest of bairns, and her age was just four ;
The solace of her mother, who found in the child
All that tied her to life—so she lived reconciled.

A widow, of sons and of daughters bereft
(Little Winnie alone to her mother was left),
She oft gazed on her treasure, and fain she would trace
A resemblance to those she had lost in her face.

Little Winnie, in infantine wisdom would sit,
Little hand clasped in mother's, her brows closely knit,
And would ask : " Mother, why do they leave us alone ?"
" Oh, my child ! they are happier where they are gone."

Then the child pondered long, and the fair little brow
Was all clouded with thought and perplexity now ;
All at once a new question sprang up in her eye :
" Then, dear mother, why do you look sorry and cry ?

6

" Have they gone far away ?   How I wish they were here !
Could we follow them there ?   We could walk, if 'twere near.
Is it high on the hill, where the sun sinks to rest ?"
Then her prattle was hushed on the sad mother's breast.

Scarce a year had slipped by ; little Winnie, alone,
Sad and weary, sat resting tired limbs on a stone ;
For her mother had gone to that land in the sky
Where the sun sinks to rest on the hill, oh, so high !

Little Winnie was trying to find out the way ;
She had walked from the morning, and all through the day,
And the hill was before her to climb, ah ! but how ?
For her poor little feet stumbled under her now.

So she laid down her sad little head on the stone,
And just asked the kind angels where mother had gone ;
And the angels for answer took Winnie away
In their strong, tender arms, with her mother to stay.

THE HAUNTED LILY.

I LEAD a sad, a lonely life;
  No voices cheer my hearth,
No happy child, no loving wife,
  No sound of song or mirth;
Not comfort even from the past,
And twilight shades are falling fast.

One night alone in all the year
  Brings saddened joy to me;
For on that night a voice I hear,
  Though no dear form I see—
A lily waving in the breeze
Wafts comfort to me through the trees.

Upon one evening in June
  I walk my garden round,
And, listening, hear in sweetest tune
  A sighing, mournful sound;
It comes from one lone, lovely spot—
The lily sings, " Forget me not."

I stand beside the bending flower,
  The stars are pale above ;
I stand for one short blessèd hour
  In converse with my love ;
The blossom tells me that she lives,
Such comfort still the lily gives.

Now flies the time, now strikes the hour—
  Nine clear loud strokes have gone ;
I turn me to my pale, pure flower,
  My *Lily*, white and wan.
In gathering shades she melts away ;
No trace is found when dawns the day.

Ah! had I known her steadfast heart,
  When first I told my tale,
We should not now be far apart,
  Though she might mock and rail.
Too late I found my life, my queen !
Too late I saw what might have been !

But she coquetted with my pain,
  She scoffed at all my woe.
I could not bear the constant strain ;
  I frowned, and let her go.
Yet while she lives, I would not die :
I live to hear my *Lily* sigh.

MOUNTAIN MARY.

Oh, have you seen the lass who dwells
   In yonder hut upon the mountain,
Hard by the rift that cleaves the fells
   Whence rushes forth a sparkling fountain?

Her eyes are clearer than the day,
   With happy laughter ever glancing;
And as she steps, a flowery way
   Springs up where naked feet go dancing.

Her bodice of a royal blue
   Withstands the stress of wind and weather;
Her petticoat of brightest hue
   Flits crimson o'er the purple heather.

She takes her pail and milking-stool—
   A cow is lowing at its tether;
Soon as the frothy pail is full
   She lifts her load as 'twere a feather.

Now Mary stops and screens her eyes
  With lifted hand ; long does she ponder ;
Then sits she down with frequent sighs.
  What ails the bonny lass, I wonder ?

She plucks a daisy part from part ;
  She pulls the petals each asunder,
To wrench an answer from its heart :
  " He comes not !"   Yet a flower *may* blunder !

So day by day at milking time,
  When evening shades begin to hover,
Sits Mary 'neath the branching lime,
  Still looking for her lagging lover.

Sad are the eyes now dimmed with tears,
  Low droops the head of Mountain Mary ;
Her throbbing heart is sore with fears
  For her true love—why does he tarry ?

She scans the footpath to the dale,
  If haply she may him discover ;
But watching is of small avail—
  No sight, no sound, save cry of plover.

And now the aged mother stands
  In anxious waiting for her daughter ;
She calls, she wrings her trembling hands,
  Upon the moor she long has sought her.

The tethered cow sends forth a wail,
  But Mary surely has forgot her ;
The frail old mother takes the pail ;
  Her failing limbs begin to totter.

The task fulfilled, again she strays
  Back to the moor in listless sorrow,
Till darkening twilight blinds her ways,
  And she must rest until the morrow.

But what is that behind the rock,
  Fast in the cleft so deep and narrow ?
A bodice blue, a crimson frock—
  A sight the mother's heart to harrow !

In helpless agony she cries,
  " My Mary ! O God, help my daughter !"
No sound is heard, no voice replies—
  Only the ever rushing water.

———————

Then, sitting down upon a stone
  To wait the succour God may send her,
She heaves a gentle sigh, a moan—
  The angels hear, and fly to tend her.

DRUMINTOUL.

I KNOW a house that stands alone
  Upon a heathery plain ;
The wind sighs round it with a moan,
  And this foretells the rain.

But on the bright and sunny days
  How sweet and fresh the air !
The mountains, half concealed in haze,
  Are grand beyond compare.

From every view-point round and round,
  As far as eye can roam,
The heather and the pine abound
  In this sweet Highland home.

Wide billowy seas of purple heath
  Reach from the very door,
Till merged in woods of pine beneath,
  And then are seen no more.

And in a hollow near the pines,
   Encircled by a wood,
A little loch half hidden shines
   In calm and tranquil mood.

But dark and stormy days will come
   When winter stalks around,
And wraps in snow the Highland home
   While lochs in ice are bound.

How dazzling then the mountain range !
   In awe we stand amazed
To see around us such a change
   Since last thereon we gazed.

We raise our hearts in thankfulness
   For such a glorious sight—
The Highland home in winter dress
   Affords us keen delight.

And now we find it hard to say
   Which dress becomes her most—
The glory of the summer day,
   Or wreathed in snow and frost.

LOCH EUNACH.

'TWAS on a day both mild and gray
  That we set out to view
Glen Eunach Head, so full of dread—
  The road to us was new.
The scent of pines was in the air ;
We drove a wagonette and pair.

Mid wood and fell, o'er hill and dell,
  Our way we quickly wound ;
Our horses strong, they sped along,
  And covered fast the ground.
Of waterfalls they took no heed,
Nor stumbled once a sturdy steed.

O'er bridges frail, that had no rail,
  Right merrily bowled we ;
Mid moor and heath, with fern beneath,
  No danger could we see ;
Till, looking down with fear and dread,
We spied the rapid torrent's bed.

The mountain side now opened wide,
  To let us enter in ;
The torrent rushed, it foamed, it gushed,
  It dazed us with its din.
Entranced, we soon forgot our fear,
So wond'rous did the scene appear!

But all at once a startled steed
  Reared up in sudden fright—
A graceful stag, with wond'rous speed,
  Came bounding into sight ;
With one huge spring the wall he cleared,
And gazed around him as we neared.

His antlers poised on graceful head,
  He stood erect, alone,
Then instantly, in sudden dread,
  With one more bound was gone ;
Midst kindly trees now hid from harm
He safely browsed without alarm.

Precipitous the mountains rise,
They seem to touch the very skies,
  Nor would they deign to yield
A foothold sure for man or beast,
Nor grass whereon a goat might feast,
  Nor flow'rets there concealed.

And we had neared Glen Eunach's Head
Ere we descried the loch's lone bed,
  Where sad and still it lay,
Its bosom dark with sullen pride,
All undisturbed by wind or tide,
  And wreathed in evening gray.

O thoughtless stranger, pause and think
Or ere you desecrate the brink
  Of this pure pebbly shore,
This silver beach made smooth by time—
Untrodden, silent, sad, sublime—
  Man never touched before!

Now, having reached our journey's end,
Our thoughts to tea and comfort tend—
  A bothy skirts the shore.
How disappointing it would be
If we should fail to find the key
  That opes the bothy door!

With eager scan we look around;
That key must promptly now be found—
  On rafter hid it lies.
We seize it quick, and in a trice
A blazing fire and all things nice
  Do greet our hungry eyes!

Farewell, proud Eunach! sad and wild,
I never more will be beguiled
   Near thy dread shores to stray.
In solemn grandeur thou dost stand;
Thou givest forth thy stern command—
   " There is no right of way!"

LOCH MORLICH.

EMERGING from the heath, we stood
Upon the margin of the wood ;
Loch Morlich, in a ruffled mood,
      Lay shimm'ring just below.
The wind was struggling with the sun,
The waters laughed to see the fun,
For now a contest had begun
      Each other to o'erthrow.

The summer heat was in the breeze,
The wind was mutt'ring through the trees,
Alert his anger to release
      And rush into the fray ;
But calmly shone the gentle rays,
Now piercing bravely through the haze ;
The breeze " took off," to our amaze —
      The sun had won the day !

The gale subdued, has ceased to blow,
And now a-fishing must we go ;
A boat lies near, a man to row,
      A rod and tackle too.

Nought more is left for us to wish,
If only we could catch some fish,
Enough to make a breakfast dish ;
    But this we cannot do.

With energy the rod we ply,
We deftly cast the tempting fly,
With all our skill and tact we try ;
    The fish refuse to bite.
So now we homeward bend the oar,
Loch Morlich, ruffled as before,
Refusing to yield up her store
    Of provender to-night.

More luck another time we hope ;
With fish so coy 'tis hard to cope.
Now soon the evening shades will slope
    Upon the mountain's breast.
Behold the sun ! he's dipping low,
One minute more, and he will go ;
He spreads o'er all a parting glow
    The while he sinks to rest.

THE WIDOW'S HUT.

A VISION sweet and homely too
In memory rises to my view—
    A hut upon the moor.
A wooden shanty, old and gray,
The roof is thatched with heath or hay;
    A figure at the door—

A woman's figure, old and bent,
Alone and frail, she's now intent
    Her cherished cow to find—
Her friend, her comfort, her support;
No company of other sort
    Has she of any kind.

With lifted hand her eyes to screen,
She looks around with anxious mien;
The cow is nowhere to be seen,
    And milking time is nigh.
Her feeble call scarce breaks the hush;
But Crummie's just behind the bush,
    And now comes saunt'ring by.

"O Crummie, little you're aware
How poor would be the widow's fare
    If aught befell to you ;
Her friend, her comfort, and her pride,
Whose daily steps she loves to guide
    Through rain, or snow, or dew."

COTTAGE OR CASTLE?

A COTTAGE, or castle? Who, then, would thus dare
To presume with such boldness these two to compare?
Where is he who in cottage contented would live
If the kindness of fortune a palace should give?

Very true, my dear friend; the conclusion is clear—
You are happier far with ten thousand a year;
There is no further question that yours is the gain,
So to argue is needless, the answer is plain.

Yet some castles have drawbacks, and this you'll admit
After candid reflection: your habits must fit
All the lordly dimensions of style and of state;
You are trammelled with forms and the cares of the great.

But now, setting aside all the cares thus entailed,
Have your riches, in any particulars, failed
To procure for you all that your heart could desire?
Or would you from castle to palace aspire?

Ah, my friend, if your soul all your wants would reveal,
It is not a desire for more greatness you feel,
But for some humble cottage, with comfort replete,
With an air of home-happiness, cheerful and sweet ;

With full time for your book, or your pen, or your brush ;
And the quietness needed, the calm and the hush ;
And the silence scarce broken by Nature alone
In the song of the birds, in the wind's gentle moan.

A VISIT TO AN ENCHANTED CASTLE.

THE year is growing old,
The night is dark and cold,
   And we are sailing on the stormy sea ;
We're nearing to the shore,
We hear the breakers roar ;
   They dash upon the shingle angrily.

At length we firmly stand
Upon the darkened land,
   And look around to see if we can find
A face that we may know
To tell us where to go—
   A welcome to these shores of any kind.

We have not long to wait,
For ere we reach the gate
   That leads to light and shelter from the storm,
A voice behind us cries,
" You're welcome !" and it tries
   To lead us to a castle bright and warm.

It says: " A carriage stands
Awaiting your commands;
    Pray enter, it will drive you to the door
Of an unique domain
Where peace and plenty reign:
    You're welcome to this hospitable shore."

So now, without delay,
We mount and drive away,
    Protected from the rawness of the air;
Ensconced within the coach,
We enter the approach—
    Our sturdy steeds a very handsome pair.

Through shrubberies we wind—
Firs, pines of every kind—
    Till suddenly a blaze of light appears;
It greets our hungry eyes,
Our every tremor flies—
    It puts to flight imaginary fears.

Our panting steeds now stop;
They've reached the steep hilltop.
    The door flies open ere we touch the bell;
Two figures forward come
To welcome to their home
    The guests whose coming they could not foretell.

In every room a fire—
What more could we desire ?
   A rich repast we find is laid for two.
Our host himself now waits ;
His wife hands in the plates,
   But keeps herself discreetly out of view.

We soon retire to rest
In this enchanted nest,
   Contented with its peacefulness profound ;
And, like the wise cuckoo,
We now, without ado,
   Appropriate the comforts we have found.

And morning brings new joys,
Kind offers of grand ploys,
   A three-mast yacht to sail in when we please ;
The coach and pair at hand,
To drive us through the land—
   Enchanting treats await us such as these.

We ponder much and long—
To whom can these belong ?
   The castle with its turrets and its towers,
The treble-masted yacht
To anchor near us brought,
   The coach and pair to drive us by the hour.

We know it cannot be
The couple whom we see
   Attending to our daily wants with care;
For silently they creep,
As if afraid to cheep;
   With deference they offer us a chair.

Mayhap the owner kind
Will still be of the mind
   To keep himself invisible—who knows?
We must respect his views,
If even he refuse
   The name of *Selma's* master to disclose.

At length a week is spent,
And we must strike our tent—
   To castle, yacht, and coach must say adieu;
The nights are cold and long,
And north-east winds are strong;
   The yacht has gone to shelter at the Row.

Now let me close my lay,
For I have said my say;
   Your turn it is to guess my riddle now;
So tell me, if you can,
The name of that kind man
   Who built his castle on the windy brow.

THE OLD FARMHOUSE.

THE sweetest corner of the earth to me
Is that old farmhouse bordering on the sea,
Where, sheltered from the gaze of curious eyes,
It stands enscreened upon a gentle rise ;
Tall larch and silver-birch, with kindly arms,
Shield its sweet, tranquil beauty from alarms.

The house itself, half smothered up in blooms,
Contains the freshest, daintiest of rooms
One could desire ; these by two daughters' care
Were built and furnished with choice things most rare ;
And naught was wanting that love could supply ;
All was arranged to please the mother's eye.

Small wonder, then, I call this corner sweet,
For every one of us would often meet
And gather there—five sons and daughters five—
All round one centre ; and we all would strive
To catch her loving smile, or take her arm
To guide her steps and lead her safe from harm.

Upon the lawn before the door there grow
Thickets of roses, planted row by row ;
Beyond, a field ; on either side a wood ;
And in the field for untold years has stood
A Druid stone, some call it ; others say
Upon a grave in olden times it lay.

The path up by the hill—the sea beneath ;
The seat upon the stone, o'ergrown with heath—
'Twas there our mother rested ; there we lay
Among the bracken, when we came this way.
The sky was blue, the days were warm and bright ;
'Twas her dear presence filled it all with light.

The honey-scented heather swept the air,
The sea danced 'neath the heated sunny glare ;
And from the distant kyles came, creeping round,
The snow-white sails of vessels outward bound ;
The mountains rose around us, rugged, grand ;
Peace, beauty, gladness filled the sea, the land.

We often sat and revelled in the day,
Till best part of an hour had slipped away—
Till evening breeze and cloud with rosy tints
Our thoughts sent homewards, giving gentle hints
Of shades descending ; then we rose to go,
Picking our steps midst bracken, sure and slow.

Sometimes our saunter led us near the sea,
Down through the field, close by the hedge, and we
Oft took a shorter path across the green,
Which brought us to the gate; from thence was seen
The cottage near the wood.   We rested there
Upon a bench to breathe the fresh sea-air.

The smiling bay below, within our reach,
Invited us to wander to the beach;
The splash of distant oar from fishing-boat,
The flying seagull's harsh discordant note,
Were all we heard; we gazed with happy glance—
Our gladdened hearts, content, with joy would dance.

Here Nature at her fairest spreads her wealth;
Here every breeze that stirs is breath of health;
The sea, half land-locked, decks her sparkling face
In tiny ripples; they each other chase;
They flow up on the sand in wreaths of foam;
They kissed our feet, and sent us, laughing, home.

The farmhouse still remains upon the rise,
The cottage stands, with brightly twinkling eyes;
The path up by the hill, the stone, the heath;
The little foot-road to the shore beneath—
All, all the haunts are there, all is the same;
Yet one is wanting, whom we need not name.

THE COTTAGE NEAR THE WOOD.

I SEE the cottage; there it stands,
Just looking o'er the yellow sands;
    Its little sparkling eyes,
Encased in windows, clearly shine,
And creepers round them intertwine—
    E'en to the roof they rise.

And from the chimney, curling smoke
Shows blue against the woods that cloak
    The cot in vivid green,
Sending a welcome far and wide
To meet us, from the wild hillside,
    E'er we ourselves are seen.

A woman's figure flits about,
With busy feet steps in and out;
    Her flutt'ring hood is white.
From time to time she scans the sea,
If in the distance there may be
    A vessel yet in sight.

Her eye, long train'd to watch each "tack"
(Her husband own'd a fishing-smack),
    Afar has spied a sail
That now the fresh'ning breeze will fill,
And bring us near, and nearer still—
    It blows full half a gale.

A flagstaff rises from the mound
Above the shore, on grassy ground,
    And thither hastens she ;
Responsive to her touch, it sends
A message, ere our journey ends,
    To cheer us on the sea.

And who so happy when, though late,
Arrived in safety, we relate
    The news from town we've brought,
As this, our faithful friend, who lives
Within the cot, and freely gives
    Her care, her love, her thought ?

Some years have passed ; she is no more,
And desolate the sunny shore
    In all its beauty stands ;
No busy feet run out and in,
No figure now sits down to spin
    With deft and careful hands.

Yet ev'ry stone around that spot
Remembers her; and there is not
  A room within those walls
That was not builded, one by one,
With needful thrift; and this was done
  By building snug " To-falls."

She lives in memory near the wood;
And still we see the snow-white hood,
  In fancy, by the door;
Or on the beach she, waiting, stands,
Among the ferns and yellow sands—
  She waits for evermore!

THE OLD MILL-WHEEL.

SILENT the old mill stands, and still;
   The broken wheel revolves no more;
The rushing mill-race flows at will;
   The idle waters freely pour
Into the river's roving breast,
   To mingle with the onward roll
That wanders restless, in the quest
   Of widening seas, beyond control.

No more we hear the mill-wheel's splash
   Resounding as in days of yore;
No more the rounding edges lash
   The foaming waters as before.
Silent the old mill stands, and still,
   Worn out with life's incessant toil;
A broken heart—not want of will—
   Has hushed the busy mill's turmoil.

Aged and frail now is the hand
   That guided once that ruined mill;
Spendthrift the son, who left his land—
   The lonely father loves him still.

Silent he stands, with eager gaze
　From cottage threshold, morn and night,
Scanning the path, the broad highways :
　At last, the much-loved form in sight !

" Father, I've come to work," he said ;
　" I've come to work, and I will try
To mill the flour and make the bread—
　To ease your toil before you die !"
Wistful the father heard the son,
　Such yearning grief was in his look.
" Too late, the sands of time are run—
　'Tis long since hope my life forsook."

Around his son his arm he flung,
　And to the mill his footsteps led ;
The battered mill-wheel, there it hung :
　" My heart is broke !" was all he said.
Silent the old mill stands, and still,
　An emblem of those wasted years ;
The river, wandering at will,
　In evening shadows disappears.

May, 1899.

KILLELLAN.

A HOUSE replete with comfort, cheerful too,
Though closed around with trees, shut in from view.
Killellan stands upon a grassy knoll,
The massive entrance guards a spacious hall ;
The doors and walls within, of purest white,
Entrap the peeping sun, reflect his light.
To this remote abode one summer day
We, by kind invitation, find our way ;
Our friends, on hospitable thoughts intent—
And seeing us on exploration bent—
Propose for us a drive upon the hill.
The road winds high and steep, and steeper still.

On looking back betimes, our route to trace,
Down to the lowest depths, as into space,
We gaze ; and, ling'ring, soon our eyes discern
A wide domain of sea-girthed heath and fern ;
The sea itself, a radiant blue expanse,
Now in quiescence lies, as in a trance.

At length the weary summit we've attained,
But not the goal we aimed at have we gained;
For at our feet, within a mile or two,
The lighthouse of the Moile comes into view.
Yet down that deep descent we dare not go,
Encumber'd by our horses and landau;
Much of our journey, and in joyous mood,
We had accomplish'd well—"'Twas all we could."
For full two hours our labouring steeds had lent
Unwearied powers to mount the steep ascent;
Their smoking flanks, distended nostrils, prove
The needful effort made our coach to move;
And with half-human eyes they stand and gaze,
As if they too, like us, in glad amaze
Were wrapt in wond'ring awe, and fain would drink
Their fill of beauty on the rocky brink.

But now we must descend, ere caught by night
While still upon this dread and giddy height.
Then, from the homeward path we soon descry
Two islands in the fading distance lie.
Oh, could we build a dwelling on this height,
'Twould truly be a cottage of delight!
No mansion should I ask, no sport demand,
But liberty to roam o'er this fair land.
Vain wish—by circumstance it is denied.
" Farewell, O beauteous sea! farewell, hillside!"

Yet one long ling'ring look or ere we leave,
To feast our eyes once more this summer's eve,
And on our souls to set sweet Nature's seal,
Some beauties from her lovely face to steal.

Upon the margin of the silver beach,
Above the shore, beyond the flow-tide's reach,
Where booming waves in times of storm resound,
Or where in calm the murmuring dirges sound,
A low gray wall, in this secluded spot,
Surrounds a piece of ground—a small square plot.
Here is God's acre, planted to the edge
With ancient stone memorials, near a hedge
That shades the crumbling wall, binds it secure,
Adorns it in the spring with blossoms pure
Of briar, convolvulus, and white hawthorn,
Transforming shades of death to bridal morn !

Here let us say adieu ; 'tis easier said
In this lone, silent nook, beside the DEAD,
Than on the breezy hill, where sun and air
Fill us with life and hope, and banish care.
" Farewell once more !"   Peace be to those who rest
Within these walls upon kind Nature's breast !

THE DESERTED HOUSE.

A HOUSE upon the height, forsaken now,
Stands grimly looking o'er the hill-head brow ;
The windows, open to admit the air,
Glower lifeless—there is no one there ;
The pathway round the house, up to the door,
Is choked with weeds, ten times tenfold, and more.

Yet here, round this same house, not long ago,
Wide fields of yellow corn waved to and fro ;
The garden path of turf of brightest green
Led to the arbour, and from thence a screen
Of high beech hedges closed the garden round ;
Within, fine roses, herbs, and fruits were found.

The house was cheerful then. 'Twas quaint and neat;
Around the door hops clung and strove to meet :
Above the porch a balcony was hung,
Half smothered in the leaves that trailed among
The roses, honeysuckle, and sweetbriar ;
They grew profuse, and clust'ring, climbed still higher.

8—2

And he who lived within, he loved the land,
And nurtured it, until, by his wise hand,
The fruitful soil burst forth, the harvest-field
Large crops of finest wheat would always yield.
He knew each yard of turf, each rose, each tree ;
His thriving herds, no kine could sleeker be.

Oft to the hillside he his way would wend
To see the reapers o'er their sickles bend.
We were his grandchildren, and many a day
We spent with him.   He let us have our way ;
He plucked for us ripe brambles from the hedge ;
He showed us nests built on the window-ledge.

Our grandmother, whose rule was no restraint,
Our aunt, who bore with us without complaint,
Nay, more, who helped us in our griefs and joys,
Who gave her time, who joined us in our ploys—
'Twas Paradise to us, what need to say,
To spend with them a long bright holiday.

Now, what a change! a doom is on the place ;
Of garden, fields or bower there's not a trace ;
Transformed from life to death, a waste they lie,
For all is now one huge new cemetery.
Its high unsightly walls run through the field
That in the days gone by rich grain would yield.

A crop of tombstones lies behind the wall
That now divides the house from fields and all.
The happy home is gone, and in its stead
The awful neighbourhood of silent dead.
No wonder, then, the house forsaken lies ;
No man comes here, until at last he dies!

1899.

THE EVERGREEN IN LONDON.

ONE day, a bright December day,
With cheerful steps I took my way;
The pale sun sent a wintry ray
   Along the busy street.
A woman on the pavement stood;
She was in want of clothes and food,
Yet was she in no saddened mood—
   She stopped a man to greet.

Her shawl was old and worn and thin,
Too frail to hold the needful pin,
Scarce fit to wrap a young babe in
   On this December day;
And she was chaff'ring with the man,
To strike a bargain was her plan.
' I'll buy it from you if I can,
   But little can I pay.'

What was it pleased the woman so
That she should her few pence forego
To make her bargain, nor would go
   Till she had gained her prize?

She tucked her babe within one arm,
And stretched the other in alarm
To seize and keep her goods from harm,
  Then laughed with gleeful eyes.

A flower-pot, and within it grew
An evergreen of sober hue—
A sturdy plant, its leaves were few,
  Yet glossy, fresh, and bright ;
This was the treasure, this the prize
That riveted the woman's eyes,
Bringing sweet visions of blue skies
  And days of pure delight.

LONDON DELIGHTS.

Hey ho! for the London delights!
For the stir, the enlivening sights!
  Hey ho! for the ploys,
  For the bustle and noise,
  For the telegraph-boys,
  The theatrical joys;
Hey ho! for the London delights!

In the country we live on the heights,
And we sigh for the town's garish lights—
  For the drives in the Row,
  Where the great ladies go,
  For the gay, gaudy show
  Moving on, to and fro;
Hey ho! for the London delights!

Now the season sets in, and the nights
Are too short for the racketing wights
  Who rush on to the fray;
  They are up and away

To the gardens by day,
And at night to the play ;
Hey ho! for the London delights!

Hey ho! for the fate that by rights
Keeps us free from such terrible plights;
From the stir and the strife,
From the war to the knife,
Where ambition is rife,—
For the pauses in life ;
Hey ho! for all worthy delights!

But Dame Fashion prepares for new flights,
All at once these enchantments she slights ;
To the country she flies,
She now wears a new guise ;
She will study the skies,
And must see the sun rise ;
Hey ho! for the country delights!

And at dawn her sweet person she dights
In pea-green, like the wood-nymphs and sprites ;
Her ambition is now
Just to milk the brown cow
With the star on its brow ;
I am told that is how
Fashion revels in country delights!

THE HOUSE IN TOWN.

OUR house in town stands side by side
  With others of its kind;
The street in front is very wide,
  Not so the street behind.

This house is tall and narrow, too,
  Our home is built of brick;
Its colour is a ruddy hue,
  The walls are far from thick.

A window-box stands on the sill
  Outside this house of ours—
'Tis filled with heather from the hill,
  Instead of winter flowers.

The neighbours who are passing by
  Do say that here reside
A truly Scottish family
  Much noted for their pride.

'Tis not of riches that we boast,
　Nor yet of cultured ways;
Beyond all these we love the most
　Dear Scotland's bonny braes.

Oft, oft the times this vision sweet
　Comes up before my eyes;
And all within, around the street,
　Forgot, unheeded lies.

My native land! Oh, could I find
　One spot on thee to rest,
All London Town I'd leave behind
　To fling me on thy breast!

OUR NEIGHBOURHOOD.

A QUESTION oft is put to me
By friends who kindly come
To call and drink a cup of tea
In this my modest home.

They live themselves in spacious halls
Nigh bordering the Park,
Where Fashion in her carriage rolls,
Where walk the men of mark.

" How do you like this neighbourhood ?"
Those kind friends ask of me.
" 'Tis healthy, we have understood ;
And what is there to see ?"

" There's nought to see but houses tall,
Built up into the sky ;
The sun might fail, the stars might fall,
But nought would reach our eye.

" Yet if from open door at night
　　We upwards search and gaze,
Our wistful eyes may find moonlight
　　When chance dispels the haze.

" And much there is to make amends,
　　And much there is of good ;
You must not think I murmur, friends:
　　I like my neighbourhood.

" Though far removed from state and pomp,
　　'Tis near the garden green,
Where age may stroll, and childhood romp—
　　There romped our Royal Queen !

" Our house in comfort may compete
　　With houses twice its size ;
Our home is wholesome, bright, and sweet,
　　Although in shade it lies.

" Our street is very broad and short,
　　It has an airy grace ;
By some, indeed, 'tis called ' The Court,'
　　To emphasize its space.

" And high it stands, full thirty feet
　　Above the parks and squares,
Where Beauty, Youth, and Fashion meet
　　In companies and pairs.

" New planted in our street there grow
  Some trees, a very few ;
The sparrows flutter to and fro,
  They never say 'adieu.'

" I often wonder will they nest
  If one day they should find
Some branches where their house might rest—
  Some leafage to their mind ?

" 'Twould pleasure me to see how skill'd
  These sparrows are ; how keen
With speed and care their nests to build
  Among the leafy green !

" Our tastes are simple, friends ; you see,
  Not much we seem to need,
By way of rout or gaiety,
  Our minds and hearts to feed.

" The quiet evenings, days of ease,
  With restful nights between—
Our neighbourhood contains all these ;
  We lead a life serene."

Our kindly friends they bow and smile,
  As if they understood ;
Their minds they cannot reconcile
  To our good neighbourhood.

MY COUNTRY HOME.

My country home is very sweet;
  It stands upon a hill ;
Its garden-walks are trim and neat;
  There is a tiny rill.

It wanders o'er a rocky bed,
  A woodland path is near ;
The waters pure are duly fed
  By Skiddaw's streamlets clear.

And all around, above, beneath,
  The beauteous mountains rise ;
Their grassy slopes are crown'd with heath ;
  They reach up to the skies.

And nestling at the mountain's base
  The Derwentwater sleeps ;
It oft is veil'd by summer haze,
  And often Nature weeps.

For, sad to tell, a rainy day
Is not uncommon here ;
And now I have no more to say—
I've said too much, I fear.

OUR FARMYARD.

A SPACIOUS, well-built square,
But empty, almost bare,
And yet the solid buildings are complete—
A pile of massive stone :
Two barns, and they alone
Do measure, end to end, full forty feet ;

A stable and a byre,
A boiler and a fire,
A piggery with doors—a lordly pen.
Upon the other side
A cart-shed broad and wide,
And last of all a bothy for the men.

An ivy, strong and tall,
That climbs o'er every wall—
In densest green it clothes the stony pile—
Into the window peeps,
And round the corner creeps
With saucy grace, in free-and-easy style.

9

Our pony, at life's close,
He still to market goes ;
His homeward journey breaks, to take a rest ;
His labouring breath is spent
Upon the steep ascent.
'Tis clear the pony now is past his best.

A donkey of fine breed,
Of use in time of need ;
Black barndoor fowls—of these we're very fond ;
A flock of turkeys white—
They are my chief delight ;
Rare ducks of brilliant plumage on the pond.

A peacock, by his tail
A rainbow might look pale ;
He struts along in stately, conscious pride.
He often walks alone ;
He cannot well condone
The dusky plumage of his dowdy bride.

Yet these, though all combined,
Or housed each with its kind,
In our farmyard make but a sorry show.
No lowing kine to feed,
No tramp of sturdy steed,
No cooing pigeons flutter to and fro.

But if I had my will
My stable I would fill
With priceless horses noted for their strength;
    The byre with two fine cows,
    White stars between their brows,
Their horns of graceful shape and proper length.

    The dairy with its pans
    Fresh filled from milkmaid's cans;
In fancy I can see her tripping in,
    Adorned with short gown blue,
    Her eyes of self-same hue,
The milk itself scarce whiter than her skin.

    With skill and care intent,
    Upon the butter bent,
To coax it into little pats of gold;
    She bustles out and in,
    Then down she sits to spin
When all the stock are gathered in the fold.

    The bleating sheep I hear,
    'Tis music to my ear;
In fancy I possess them all—each one!
    And yet I must confess
    To be content with less
Is very easy, when all's said and done.

THE HAWTHORN-TREE.

SHOULD some kind fairy give to me
The power to choose what kind of tree
My woodland pathways might adorn,
I'd choose o'er all the sweet hawthorn,
When, wreath'd in blooms of summer snow,
The scented boughs waft to and fro.

But scant the time those blooms remain ;
A few short weeks, 'tis all we gain
Of fragrance!   Yet there's something left—
We're not of all at once bereft ;
For every spray of white enshields
The coral clusters that it yields.

No longer robed in mantle white,
The thorn now stands with beads bedight ;
Her dress of such a brilliant sheen,
She shyly blushes to be seen ;
So modestly she holds her head,
As if ashamed to know it red.

Now winter comes with icy breath,
Condemning all the leaves to death ;
The foliage falls—oh, sad distress !
There's nought but berries now for dress ;
Still hanging temptingly on high,
They catch the hungry warbler's eye.

The thorn, resigned, has now begun
To yield her jewels one by one ;
She sheds her berries ripe and red,
Content to see the hungry fed ;
Denudes herself of all she's got
To satisfy the thievish lot.

Then who will question now my choice
Since every season lifts a voice
To sing the praises of this tree—
Her great superiority ?
She feeds the hungry, cheers the sad,
And makes the country waysides glad !

THE UNFRUITFUL GARDEN.

Most tuneful folks who sing
Much praise desire to bring
To bear upon the subject of their song ;
    And this is only right,
    No audience could delight
In list'ning to unworthy lays for long.

And yet I fain would try
To bring before your eye
A vision of the garden I possess ;
    It occupies my mind ;
    Fit words I cannot find—
Unfruitful, joyless, full of dreariness.

No flow'rs will blossom there,
No gard'ner's skill or care
Can coax the trees to yield their luscious fruit ;
    He scarce can raise a trace
    Of vegetable race—
Of cauliflow'r, asparagus, beetroot.

'Tis borne upon my mind
No garden so designed
To thwart all expectation should exist ;
   To clear it of its weeds,
   Its fruitless trees and seeds,
A duty is, on which I must insist.

   'Twould surely be a shame
   Should I my garden blame
For want of power to grow the finer gear ;
   Behold ! from garden rough
   To lawn of velvet turf
Transformed—it's true vocation now is clear.

   With tennis-ball and net,
   With nice new croquet set,
Its surface now so cheerfully bedight,
   My garden can produce
   Rich harvests of much use,
For shouts of gladness ring from morn to night !

THE FOUNTAIN.

THE fountain sings to me
When I sit beneath the tree,
While it prattle, prattle, prattles all the day.
It sings of woods and streams ;
I can see them in my dreams,
While it trickle, trickle, trickles by the way.

It bids me hear the breeze
Coming whistling through the trees,
And it ripple, ripple, ripples in its play ;
Its music does entrance,
It invites me to the dance
In a merry, merry, merry roundelay.

It bids me look around
Over lawn and mossy ground,
While it babble, babble, babbles glad and gay ;
It says the fairies soon
Will hold revel with the moon
While it sparkle, sparkle, sparkles night and day.

It tells me how they fly
When the dawn breaks in the sky,
Midst its weeping and entreating them to stay;
But fairies can't delay,
When they see the break of day
They must hasten, hasten, hasten fast way.

And now the song is sung,
And the matin bells are rung,
Yet I listen, listen, listen to the spray;
The fountain still flows on
From the evening to the dawn,
And I bow with bended knee and humbly pray.

THE CROQUET LAWN.

IT chanced one day that we
The need began to see
To have a croquet lawn on our domain ;
But where to find the spot,
For not one rood we'd got
That could be called a proper grassy plain.

Beneath the hill we found
A piece of level ground—
Or such it seemed when measured by the eye.
Our gard'ner did his best,
With spirit-level test ;
His courage failed him, still, he could but try.

And now six weeks have gone,
Six men have laboured on
In turning up the stiff and stony sod ;
Their shovels meet hard rocks,
In huge ungainly blocks,
Yet six times six of weary weeks they plod.

To blasting they resort,
A quite exciting sport,
A relaxation from their daily toil ;
The winter thus is spent
On our experiment,
Yet much I fear 'twill prove for us a foil.

A long, long year has passed,
And now in hope at last
We view the ground—the lawn is near complete ;
A grassy bank has grown
(No trace of rock or stone)—
A level plain, in length near ninety feet.

A shelter-house we build,
With seats and table filled,
From which to view the players at our ease ;
And should our friends prove kind—
For them it was designed—
We'll meet them there as often as they please.

1898.

THE OLD "GRANDFATHER" CLOCK.

He stands in the hall, the old clock, by the door;
  He is stately and solemn and grim ;
His face full of wisdom, his head full of lore,
  We're always consulting with him.
So constant his motion, so rapid his pace,
Yet somehow he never moves out of his place.

He is courtly and polished to one and to all,
  He is ever obliging and kind ;
To those who inquire, be they tiny or tall,
  His manner is truly refined.
He never refuses to give a reply ;
His voice is delib'rate, yet time seems to fly.

In low, steady accents, so staid and sedate,
  He tells us to work while 'tis day ;
He warns us through life we must never be late
  For labour, appointments, or play.
In tones loud and sounding he speaks by the hour :
"Oh, catch fleeting moments while still in your power!"

Such wisdom contained in his spare rigid frame
　Does almost imbue him with life—
Entitles him to the philosopher's fame,
　Undying and gained without strife.
Through long ling'ring years he still goes on his way;
He is never in haste, yet he can't brook delay.

But who in the ages to come will reveal,
　In reading his face o'er again,
What weariness this poor old clock must then feel—
　Dejection, rheumatics, and pain?
Alas! not exempt from a fate we deplore,
His fame still lives on, but the *clock* is no more!

TO THE LAKE.

WATER, silver-dashed,
  Fed by rapid river ;
By the oarsman lashed
  Till your ripples quiver.
Calm you lie and lone,
  Bosomed in the mountains,
Like a precious stone
  Washed by many fountains.

Cloudlets, hills, and trees,
  Here and there a palace,
On your face one sees ;
  Rainbow-skies and valleys,
Traced with fairy's paint,
  Touched by fairy's feather :
While we look they faint—
  Gone, all gone together.

When the evening veils
   Nature in her gauzes,
Shades reveal new tales
   While the twilight pauses ;
Magic lights are seen
   On your surface glancing,
When the night's pale queen
   Sends her rays a-dancing.

But another mood
   Lurks behind your gladness,
Storms and tempests rude
   Lashing you to madness.
Then, with cruel joy,
   Wicked fiends possess you ;
Human life destroy—
   Nor does this distress you !

Smiling once again—
   Passion now is over ;
But the loss and pain
   You will ne'er discover.
Tempting heedless youth,
   Cold and calm, unfeeling,
With a show of truth
   Hearts and bodies stealing.

Water, silver-dashed,
   Fed by rapid river ;
By the oarsman lashed
   Till your ripples quiver ;
Jewelling the plain,
   By vast heights surrounded—
Lies no hint of pain
   In your depths unsounded.

A REFLECTION.

THE sweet secret of happiness, where does it lie—
In hiding, or can it be seen by the eye?
To seek it must we into far countries roam?
Or does it lie quietly waiting at home?

Will it yield to our pursuit, or will it evade
All our anxious endeavours, and then slowly fade
Into nothingness, just as we've grasped a new thought?
" Can this secret of pleasure be possibly bought
By the man who is rich?   Is it only for him
Who can easily gratify every new whim?"

Then the chase I relinquish, no secret I'll find;
To a colourless fate I must now be resigned.
All the real needs of life I must sturdily face;
With a cheerful endurance must " run the good race."
But now mark what a prospect has gladdened my eyes:
" 'Tis the secret long hidden—how open it lies!"

April, 1899.

ODE TO CONTENTMENT.

CONTENTMENT, gracious virtue! Blest is he
Who through life's journey has a friend in thee;
Content am I with what Fate has in store,
If thou, Contentment, stand'st within my door;
Should wealth pour down its favours on my way,
My thanks to Fortune I will humbly pay.

Let not the brimming fulness of my cup
Increase desire for more than fills it up;
Nor let me be o'erbalanced by the weight
Of worldly goods bestowed by fickle Fate
Not always for deserts or due rewards,
But oft through chance that circumstance affords,
And oft, when absent, it had done less ill,
Than, in possession, stifling work and will.

Befriend me when the gray and cheerless day
Drags its long length, and not one single ray

Of sunlight penetrates the dreary gloom
To flicker round the corners of my room ;
Thy presence then shall sweetly shed the light
So needful to my jaded, weary sight,
And calmly I will wait till Fortune brings
The dawn of better times upon her wings.

TO MY FRENA.

Companion of my daily walks and drives,
   Her eye prepared to take in all she sees—
This friend of mine each view to find contrives,
   The fields, the lakes, the rivers, hamlets, trees;
Her searching eye so eager is and keen,
She never once forgets to note the scene!

Thus stored with recollections so complete—
   Her memory of the most retentive kind—
She tells of bygone times with joys replete.
   How rare a friend! possessed of such a mind.
My Frena! true companion, it is you
Who cheer my days with visions ever new!

PRAYER TO NIGHT.

I GAZE on thy beauty, O wonderful Night!
Thou art cloth'd in the softest effulgence of light;
Thou hold'st in thy bosom, half hidden from sight,
The moon, whose pale radiance grows rapidly bright.
Oh, fain would I stray to some far-reaching height!
To touch thy soft moonbeam would be such delight!

Then lift me up tenderly, lay me to rest
On soft fleecy cloudlets enfolding thy breast;
So lull me to sleep in the sweet-scented air,
And waft to the heavens my poor humble prayer.
Soon morning shall come with the radiance of day,
And clothe me with wings that will bear me away.

SHADOW LAND.

Who can they be who come in early morn—
A company forlorn ?
In silence they advance to greet the sun,
His rising has begun ;
They slowly creep as if afraid to bring
Their humble, lowly homage to their king.

They prostrate lay their length upon the ground,
They utter not a sound ;
Their sovereign bids them rise, and now they stand
Awaiting his command ;
Though gaunt and large they loom before my eyes,
I marvel how they lessen much in size.

His mandate they receive ; I wonder still,
For at his powerful will
Again they lengthen out and steal along,
And lo ! the evensong,
How sweet it sounds o'er all the shadow land !
The list'ning host creep on, a ghostly band.

THE SILVER LINING.

Clouds, clouds upon clouds, they come sweeping along,
And still they come breathing their sad sullen song,
From morning till night, and from night until morn :
Oh, dark was the day upon which I was born !

Clouds, clouds upon clouds, they are filling the air
With sorrow and brooding, and trouble and care ;
They heed not the frailties of poor feeble man—
Think nothing of short'ning his brief little span.

The sun, man's deliv'rer, is shining behind,
Yet not one slight trace of his light can we find.
When, when shall the dawn of the morning arise ?
Where, where shall I find a blue rift in the skies ?

I see not one signpost upon life's dark road,
While, stumbling, my weary feet seek an abode ;
I still seek the home that was promised to all
Who fight the fight bravely and strive not to fall.

My strength is exhausted, I sink by the way ;
My senses are failing, I can't even pray ;
But one look I give to the heavens above.
Lo! the rift is appearing—the clouds slowly move!

As one by one parting they show the blue sky,
They drift along faster ; I can just descry
A lining of silver ; 'tis showing behind.
There, there is the promise—the cloud silver-lined !

SHADOWS.

How charming the slope of the hillside when dress'd
In the soft ev'ning shade that trails out from the west,
　　Its beauty enhanced, not concealed !
More pleasing to sight than the strong mid-day light
That levels the landscape when glaringly bright,
　　In which each defect is reveal'd.

So life has its shadows, our pathway they've crossed ;
Unwarn'd, into seas of distress we were toss'd
　　In an anguish of grief and despair ;
But faith's outstretch'd arm bore us up beyond harm,
The clouds are now passing, we feel no alarm—
　　We are free'd from our burden of care !

The life that is chequer'd with sunshine and shade
Is stronger to fight and is quicker to aid,
　　In the battle of oncoming years,
Than the life that's been spent on its own good intent,
While basking in sunshine, on pleasure still bent,
　　Without a suspicion of shade.

WHO CAN GUESS?

Who can guess our thoughts ? They wander
  Limitless in wild career ;
Darting here and there, o'er yonder
  Realm of space, and know no fear.

None can guess our thoughts ! We ponder
  Over things remote and strange ;
But our minds grow fond and fonder
  Of this never-ending change.

Fancy rears a stately palace,
  Fairy "castle in the air ";
Thither fly our thoughts for solace
  From life's daily cark and care.

There we find ourselves attended
  By the spirits of our dreams ;
Every wish there comprehended ;
  There we drink of Lethe's streams.

" Hark, a noise!"   'Tis but the rattle
 Of the dying ember's fall;
Vanish'd is our fairy castle—
 Gone our dream beyond recall!

THE LION'S SHARE.

THE lion's share by all is sought ;
Both man and beast for it have fought ;
They all concur in this, 'tis plain—
The largest share, the greatest gain.

But some exceptions must be made ;
We may not all mankind degrade
To such a depth of selfishness—
There are a few content with less.

A few, a very few there are
Who covet not the lion's share—
Whose neighbour's good is first their care ;
Kind thoughts and gifts they have to spare.

They find in this delight so pure,
It is for them a gain more sure
Than lion's share of worldly pelf,
And constant thought of nought but self.

Herein is seen a difference
Which can be shown in man's defence—
A diff'rence we are pleased to trace
'Twixt man and tailless monkey race.

Yet savants say there is a tie
Between us and the beasts that die—
Whose soulless bodies soon must lie
Forgotten in eternity.

Then let us have a care to see
That we not over-mindful be
To gain the lion's share in life—
This only leads to useless strife.

It holds our higher nature down,
And blunts the sense of right and wrong ;
And thus, we see, the bravest man
Is he who lives as best he can :

To keep his soul alive and pure
By kindly acts that will endure.
The love he shows can never die—
Proclaims his immortality.

MORNING.

PALE morning rises softly, fair, and sweet;
   She hides her glory in a trailing mist,
And, slow unveiling, bathes her lingering feet
   In dew that night's cold lips have gently kissed.

Arrayed complete in pure and radiant beams,
   She smiles a blessing on earth's waking breast;
While drowsy man, scarce roused from heavy dreams,
   In shamed amaze, a laggard stands confessed.

EVENING.

AFTER A NOVEMBER STORM.

A STILLNESS broods upon the land, no sound
   But rush of running water breaks the calm ;
The tempest's fury spent, a peace profound
   Steals on the soul like sweet and soothing balm.

An evening sky is darkening in the west,
   Black clouds trail slowly, and behind their edge
A newborn-moon now shyly shows her crest,
   Then sinks behind the mountain's rock-bound ledge

THE MARKET.

WEATHER stands at "fair,"
Bright the sunny morning;
Vendors throng the square,
Each his wares adorning.
Side by side they stand,
Honest in their dealing;
All the working band
Do show a friendly feeling.

Hark! the ancient bell
Ten clear strokes is ringing;
Merchandise to sell,
Dames and maids are bringing.
Trip, trip, trip they come,
Each with basket laden;
Hear the happy "hum"
Of chattering wife and maiden.

Each her produce brings,
    Proud to show her sample—
Butter, eggs, good things,
    Cheese and cherries ample.
Now, on business bent,
    Customers arriving;
See them all intent,
    In eager service striving.

"Come! oh, come and buy!
    Test our goods and rations;
You have but to try.
    Fruits of foreign nations!
Home-grown roots are here,
    Best of garden growing;
None can call them dear—
    The pick of this year's sowing.

" We can well supply
    Woollen goods and cotton;
Glasses for the eye—
    Nothing is forgotten.
Dainty snow-white ware,
    Cups of chaste designing,
Vases, plates, most rare,
    Both use and grace combining.

Buyers young and old
  Come to spend their earnings ;
Parting from their gold
  With reluctant yearnings.
Many hours are spent
  While they gaze and ponder ;
Anxious brows are bent—
  From stall to stall they wander.

Now the sun sinks low ;
  Market-day is over.
Homeward all they go,
  Merry lass and lover.
For good luck in trade
  Heart and burden lightens.
Suns may sink and fade ;
  Hope's star the pathway brightens.

THE LADY'S RAKE.*

A LEGEND.

BLACK and brooding rise the mountains,
  Mists and vapours shroud their height;
Silent hang the frozen fountains
  Sleeping through drear winter's night.
Bare and leafless hang the willows
  Round the lordly island home,
Sporting with the mimic billows,
  Rippling into wreaths of foam.

Stately stands the lonely castle,
  Half concealed by naked trees;
Sombre pines with many a tassel
  Waving in the wintry breeze.
Joy for ever has departed
  From that house; its lord has gone!
And a lady, broken-hearted,
  Weeps within its walls alone.

* The Lady's Rake is a cleft in the hillside at Derwentwater.

11—2

See, a hasty horseman carries
  Woeful tidings to the isle ;
Tearless now the lady tarries,
  Sobbing in her heart the while.
Fortitude her sorrow chastens ;
  Never shall her courage fail,
Though the breathless horseman hastens
  Open-mouthed, to tell his tale.

" Derwentwater's lord is taken,
  Captured in the deadly fight ;
All his righteous soul is shaken,
  Warring for his cause—the right !
Stripped of coat, he stood uncumbered,
  Better thus to strike the foe ;
But his men were far outnumbered,
  Yet they gave them blow for blow.

" London Tower is now the dwelling
  Of my lord and master dear ;
And my heart and brain are swelling
  With an angry pain and fear.
To a fading hope now clinging,
  He is prisoned with despair !"
Clear the lady's voice sounds, ringing,
  " I will find him even there !"

Pale, distracted, still she lingers
    For an instant in the hall ;
Then, with hasty, trembling fingers,
    Throws a mantle over all.
Swiftly o'er the drawbridge stealing
    In the gloom of early dawn,
Soon she stands alone, scarce feeling
    That her joy—her peace has gone !

On the highway there is peril.
    Can she scale the frowning rock,
Looming dark and dripping, sterile—
    Threatening her way to block ?
Yea, the Countess Derwentwater,
    Strengthened by her mighty love,
Flies untended ; those who sought her
    Saw her climb the heights above,

Daring not to look behind her,
    Leaving in her hasty flight,
Hanging midway, as reminder,
    Kerchief pure as snow is white.
When, the painful journey ended,
    She has found her lord at last,
Seeking now a King offended,
    Prostrate she herself has cast,

Begging for her dear lord's pardon,
　Deep despair in every tone.
But the King his heart does harden,
　Rudely bidding her "Begone!"
Every effort unavailing,
　Will the Countess pine and die?
No; her love is still unfailing.
　To her lord she now must fly!

In the prison-cell she meets him.
　"Courage, husband!" is her wail.
But the anguished eye that greets him
　Tells its own sad, fateful tale.
Watching from her lonely casement,
　Waiting the dread hour in fear,
Lo! she sees in sad amazement
　Derwentwater Lights* appear!—

Sees a strange weird glow suffusing
　Skies aflame with brilliant gleams,
Darting sudden fires, diffusing
　O'er the land their fitful gleams.
Omen of a dire disaster,
　Heaven's wrath it must portend:
Derwentwater's lord and master
　Bravely meets his bitter end!

* The Aurora Borealis is said to have been seen on the night of the
execution of Lord Derwentwater, and is still called by the country
people "Lord Derwentwater's Lights."

WAR!

Our country is at war!*   The reign of peace
  Is meantime ended, and brave England still
  Keeps sending forth in thousands at her will
The strongest of her sons, nor do they cease.
They haste to foreign shores to scale the height
  Nigh inaccessible.   The steepest hill
  Is nought to them ; they rush, the foe to kill !
And Britain's sons of weeping mothers fight !
They fight from dawn till falls the dragging day;
  And some are slain ere they can hear the cry
That would have soothed their dying as they lay;
  For some are left to shout, "Oh, victory!"
Brave sons !   True men !   Our country owes to you
A debt too deep to render you your due !

* The Battle of Elandslaagte, fought on Saturday, October 21, 1899,

THE TRANSVAAL WAR, 1899.

BATTLES OF ELANDSLAAGTE AND NICHOLSON'S NEK.

Hear ye, all nations,
  Sound it afar,
Lend lamentations—
  England makes war !
Heavily, heavily
  Britain has lost ;
Little she reckoned
  On what it would cost.

It is her honour
  She must defend ;
Taking upon her
  Thousands to send
Into the heart
  Of the turmoil and toil—
Throwing to Boers
  The sons of her soil !

Rushing the battle,
  Scaling the hill ;
(How the shells rattle !)
  Higher up, still !
Now in the thick of it,
  Dashing through fire ;
Brave men—oh, think of it—
  Fight and expire !

*   *   *   *

Fatal the onrush
  Charging the foe ;
Recked not the ambush
  Waiting below.
Trapped by the enemy
  Into the snare ;
Captured by treachery,
  All unaware !

"Call this ' disaster ' ?
  'Tis but a mistake ;
Send us help faster
  Fresh conquests to make.
See the troops landing—
  Brave Buller has come !
Legions commanding,
  Sound bugle and drum."

Britain victorious
  Stands in her pride ;
Honest and glorious—
  Nothing to hide !
Nought but the wail
  Of the mothers and wives—
Nought but the loss
  Of the brave heroes' lives !

THE END.

BILLING AND SONS, PRINTERS, GUILDFORD.